"Die with your axes red!"

Cormac shook the priest lightly. The dying man roused, as a man waking slowly from deep sleep.

"Go," he whispered. "They have done their worst to me. But you—they will lap you round with evil spells—they will break your body as they have shattered mine. They will seek to break your souls as they would have broken mine but for my everlasting faith in our good Lord God.

"He will come, the monster, the high priest of infamy, with his legions of the damned—listen!" The dying head lifted. "Even now he comes! May God protect us all!"

Cormac snarled and wheeled about. Aye, something was coming down one of the smaller corridors which opened into that wider one. "Close the ranks!" snarled Wulfhere. "Make the shield-wall, wolves, and die with your axes red!"

The Vikings quickly formed into a half-moon of steel, surrounding the dying priest and facing outward, just as a hideous horde burst from the dark opening into the comparative light. In a flood of black madness and red horror their assailants swept upon them. Most of them were goat-like creatures, that ran upright and had human hands and faces frightfully partaking of both goat and human. But among their ranks were shapes even more fearful. And behind them all, luminous with an evil light in the darkness of the winding corridor from which the horde emerged, Cormac saw an unholy countenance, human, yet more and less than human. Then on that iron wall of shields the noisome horde broke.

THE ROBERT E. HOWARD LIBRARY

Cormac Mac Art

Forthcoming:
Kull
Solomon Kane
Bran Mak Morn
Eons of the Night
Trails in Darkness
Beyond the Borders

CORMAC MAC ART

ROBERT E. HOWARD

BAEN

CORMAC MAC ART

Introduction, Note on the Text, "The Land Toward Sunset" and "Tigers of the Sea" from section 6, "I have a better plan, Cormac" (noninclusive), copyright © 1995 by David A. Drake. "Tigers of the Sea," "Swords of the Northern Sea" and "The Temple of Abomination" (long version) copyright © 1974 by Glenn Lord, Administrator to the Estate of Robert E. Howard. "The Temple of Abomination" (short version) © 1995 by Alla Ray Morris. "The Night of the Wolf" copyright © 1969 by Glenn Lord, Administrator to the Estate of Robert E. Howard.

A Baen Books Original

Baen Publishing Enterprises
P.O. Box 1403
Riverdale, NY 10471

ISBN: 0-671-87651-1

Cover art by C. W. Kelly

First printing, March 1995

Distributed by Simon & Schuster
1230 Avenue of the Americas
New York, NY 10020

Printed in the United States of America

DEDICATION

To Glenn Lord
Who over the years has done more to bring
Robert E. Howard's work to a wide
audience than any other single person.

CONTENTS

Introduction ix

A Note on the Text.................................... xiii

THE LAND TOWARD SUNSET 1

TIGERS OF THE SEA................................ 73

SWORDS OF THE NORTHERN SEA 123

THE NIGHT OF THE WOLF..................... 157

THE TEMPLE OF ABOMINATION 191

THE TEMPLE OF ABOMINATION
    (outline) 205

to guide it. Cormac back-slashed through the savage's throat, choking his scream into a gurgle.

Cormac drew the dagger from his belt and waded

INTRODUCTION:

ANCIENT HISTORY

The late Karl Edward Wagner and I are two of a number of writers of our generation—we were born in 1945—who started writing in high school because we'd run into the works of Robert E. Howard.

Oh, we read a lot of other things also. H. P. Lovecraft made quite an impact when we could find him, which wasn't that easy. I had a copy of the Avon collection *Cry Horror* (a retitling of *The Lurking Fear and Other Stories*) and anthologies occasionally included a Lovecraft story, but when I was 16, I'd probably read more Lovecraft pastiches by August Derleth than real Lovecraft.

The fantasy and science fiction field was much smaller in the '50s and '60s. It was possible to read everything that came out (or everything that made it to a newsstand near where you lived: this is also before the appearance of malls with one or two chain bookstores in every community). Science fiction included paperbacks of Jules Verne, fantasy meant *Dracula* as well as *Conan the Conqueror*. There were new editions of novels from the '20s and '30s as well as "modern"—John W. Campbell—edited—SF from the '40s and new work by present-day giants like Poul Anderson and Gordon R. Dickson.

A very eclectic mix, enormous in scope if not in volume; but it was Robert E. Howard who made us want to *write*.

I can't tell you why that should have been the case. Howard had exceptional narrative ability. That encourages people to read him, but it's not the same thing as getting them to write. Besides, there were many fine storytellers in the fantasy and SF fields then (I'm afraid that's far less the case today).

It's true that most other fantasy and SF written up to the time Howard committed suicide in 1936 is unreadable today. (Try S. P. Meek, a very popular author of the period. Fred Pohl once told me that in his opinion Meek was the worst author ever to write in the field, and I didn't argue with him.) That's of historical interest, but it didn't matter to me in 1960 when I was encountering many fine storytellers of a slightly later period. Henry Kuttner and Eric Frank Russell are two of my favorites who, in their very different ways, were Howard's equals as storytellers.

Kuttner and Russell made me want to read more SF and fantasy; Howard made me want to write as well as read. My first real short story was a heroic fantasy written for my high school creative writing class when I was 17. It wasn't a Howard pastiche, but it wouldn't have been written had I not read *Conan the Conqueror* and a smattering of other REH stories, mostly in the Conan series.

My guess, and it's just a guess, as to why Howard made a writer of me (and Karl, and others) is that Howard honestly believed the basic truth of the stories he was telling. It's as if he'd said, "This is how life really was lived in those former savage times!"

Was he right? Well, truth is a slippery commodity. Howard wasn't a scholar (though he had far more formal education than most of his contemporaries in the field, Lovecraft in particular). He read voraciously, both non-fiction histories and the adventure pulps which, at the high end, were written to a respectable standard of accuracy and erudition.

I would have to say that the viewpoint of a man who put a bullet through his own head at age 30 was likely to be biased toward bleakness; but many of the periods about which Howard wrote were bleak enough in all conscience. He may well have had a better grasp of the mindset of a 6th century reiver than would a detached academic.

But it wasn't the absolute truth of what Howard described that moved me. It was his belief and *my* belief in that truth. That's what caused me to put first an echo of his truth on paper and later, after I had experience of my own, my own visions of truth.

I've said that Robert E. Howard's work in general led me to become a writer. Cormac Mac Art specifically enabled me to write my first novel.

In 1977 I'd been selling fiction for a decade, but I'd never gotten more than a couple chapters into a novel. I didn't know how to write a work of more than 10,000 words.

There was a boom in heroic fantasy at the time, sparked and largely fueled by the works of Robert E. Howard. In addition to bringing a lot of previously unavailable Howard to print, various Howard characters were farmed out to other writers to do pastiches. A pastiche is a work in the style of another author, using themes and often characters from the original author's oeuvre. My story in this collection, "The Land toward Sunset," is an example of a pastiche.

Andy Offutt was picked to continue the *Cormac Mac Art* series. Andy was a very experienced novelist with a great affection for Howard's work, but his strength was not in the direction of densely-plotted adventure fiction of the sort Howard himself wrote.

Andy asked me and at least one other writer to do plot outlines for him to turn into Cormac novels. Andy would pay and credit us depending on the degree of our involvement in the final product.

So I spent the next five months researching aspects of history, culture and war in the Dark Ages. The plot grew slowly but very steadily. Because the plot was for another writer who wouldn't have the original sources available, I described matters in considerable detail. The final version of the plot was over 15,000 words in length.

And Andy didn't need it. I'd been so long about the business that events had moved beyond me. Andy offered to pay me a kill fee, but by that time I was just as glad that I didn't have to give the plot over to somebody else. I wanted to use it to write a novel myself.

That's exactly what I did. My first novel, *The Dragon Lord*, follows my Cormac outline with no difference except the names of the characters. The most important part of the experience was that I'd learned a technique by which I could write further novels. Not everybody needs to work from a detailed plot outline—but *I* do.

Helping edit this series of Robert E. Howard's non-Conan work for Baen Books has been more a pleasure than a job. It's also been a recognition of the debt I owe Howard.

If one of the results is that new readers decide that they want to tell stories themselves, then that debt will have been paid in full ... with no small interest accruing to Baen Books, a publisher to whom story values still matter.

Dave Drake
Chatham County, NC

A NOTE ON THE TEXT

None of the stories in this collection were published during Robert E. Howard's lifetime. "Swords of the Northern Sea" and "The Night of the Wolf" were completed but unsold when Howard died in 1936. They represent his attempt in the late '20s to break into the adventure pulps, which paid better than *Weird Tales*, his usual market.

"The Land toward Sunset" is entirely pastiche, though the themes and setting will be familiar to other Howard fans.

Glenn Lord found incomplete two of the stories here included when he became agent for the Howard estate. Glenn believes that Howard simply quit writing and put the stories aside; others have suggested that Howard finished the stories but the final pages were later lost. (On this as with most questions regarding Howard's works, I prefer to follow Glenn's opinion.)

"Tigers of the Sea" is clearly a rough draft (in manuscript, the name of one of the major characters changes between the first and second sections). The last words Howard wrote in the story are these in section VI:

"Wait," said Donal. "I have a better plan, Cormac."

    I wrote the remainder of the story. Howard didn't leave a plot outline—and indeed, it's possible he threw the manuscript aside because he didn't see any useful place for the story to go after that point. There's a long tradition of posthumously completing an unfinished story—there've been any number of completions of *The Mystery of Edwin Drood* since Dickens died, for example, including the one Dickens himself dictated through a medium—but quite frankly I was uncomfortable with the job. I hope that my addition to the story is interesting in its own right, but I truly don't know how Howard planned to complete "Tigers."

    "The Temple of Abomination" is a different matter. Although the story was unfinished in final form, Glenn Lord has found a short version of the piece which is effectively a plot outline. Instead of completing the long version of the story, I've let it stand as Howard wrote it—but with the short version, the outline, appended. I find the outline to have an eerie power on which I don't care to intrude. Besides, there's enough David Drake in this volume already.

—DAD

THE LAND TOWARD SUNSET

THE LAND TOWARD SUNSET

David Drake

"Stroke!" bellowed Cormac Mac Art from the starboard bow oar. Stormwinds shredded his voice—even *his* voice—before the words carried down the thirty pairs of Viking rowers.

On the quarterdeck the captain, Wulfhere Skull-splitter, leaned vainly with all his bearlike might against the steering oar. The corposant glowed on the peak of Wulfhere's helmet, on the tips of the powerful Danish bow he slung even at this venture across his chest, and on the hairs of his red beard blowing like a bonfire in the storm.

"Stroke!" Cormac cried. The wind clawed the command and braided it into the mindless shriek of a seabird, another sport of the storm. He should have saved his effort for the oar, nineteen feet of straight-grained pine, salt-crusted and fighting the Gaelic reiver's strength as if it too were viciously alive.

They'd gambled against the weather, hoping to strike Saxon steadings in a season when no raiders were expected. The weather had thrown the higher dice, blasting out of the northeast with a laughing fury.

That storm was natural. It had tossed and buffeted

the pirates, flinging them along a course the wind-gods chose, but the ship was well-found and well-manned. They would have ridden it out in time, then made their way back to England and plundered with violence redoubled for their oar-strained muscles.

Now winds and currents gripped to drag the vessel straight to Hell. Doom's glowing portal gaped to star-board, closer every heartbeat despite anything the tired oarsmen could do.

"Stroke!" Cormac pulled, his feet braced against a strake and his buttocks rising from the sea chest which supported him on the recovery stroke. The bow oar, longer and therefore heavier than those of the lower-riding stern, flexed dangerously against its deer-antler thole.

Where nothing but storm should be, a purple-green, unnatural hoop of light a hundred feet in diam-eter drew the vessel. The rising arc towered unmoved despite the gale; the lower half glowed through the white-capped sea. Wind and water roared toward the hoop's hazy throat, bearing the raiders with them.

The Danes were stark Vikings who had faced death a hundred times in the dance of swords and axes. Cormac had thought no disaster could cow them, but this Hell-sent apparition had crushed many of the men to apathy. They sat on their sea chests, watching with dull eyes as their doom approached.

Even so, at least a score of the pirates were rowing, men nearly as strong as Cormac himself. Their oars would have driven the supple longship through calm seas faster than a man on shore could walk. For all their efforts, the vessel continued to slip sideways toward the glowing circle.

Wulfhere leaned outward to fight the counterthrust on his steering oar, a ten-foot slab carved from the heartwood of a mighty oak. The oar's deep bite from the roiling sea was not enough to overcome the uncanny pull of the current. Wulfhere's mouth was open, bellowing defiance to whatever god or demon gripped his ship and crew. The quavering corposant that now clung to all the vessel's peaks and edges was itself stained by the hoop's purple-green light.

"Stro—"

But before the vain command was flung to the wind's mockery, Cormac saw Wulfhere—his oath-brother, his companion of a score of bloody battles in which they two stood back to back and defied the world; his *friend*—lurch over the rail of the long-ship. It was not the oak which had given way before the Dane's desperate might, but rather the knot of tough spruce root which bound the oarshaft to the wort in the vessel's side.

Still clutching the tiller, his face bearing a look of surprise, Wulfhere pitched head first into the waves. For all the Dane had been born at the water's edge and had sailed the pirate seas since before he was twelve, he could no more swim than he could fly.

Vikings shouted in muffled consternation at this new disaster on the brink of a still-greater one. Cormac dropped his oar and mounted the rail. Like his friend, he was fully armed. This blind storm could have swept them together with another ship, and all ships were foes in these Viking seas. The survivors would have been the crew which had prepared for instantaneous slaughter.

Now Cormac's sword, his steel cap, and the coat of fine ring mail which had protected a Roman officer in the days before the empire's ruin were only so much weight and hindrance to his movements. No matter.

The Gael went into the sea in a clean dive, his eyes fixed on his sinking friend. The Dane still gripped the steering oar, but his armored weight was too great for the oak to buoy to the surface.

Cormac reached Wulfhere in three powerful strokes. He grasped the collar of the Dane's iron-scaled corselet. The current was as fierce as a millrace.

For a moment the circle of light was a glowing bar above and beneath the struggling pair. Then the apparition closed behind them and Cormac felt an instant of vertigo. He fell toward nothing at all.

The transition from nowhere to *some*where was as abrupt as thought. There was no impact, only the shock of cold stone flooring beneath Cormac and awareness that purple-green light streamed through the pillared side-aisles and clerestory windows of a vast building.

Cormac scrambled to his feet. Wulfhere rose simultaneously, iron-shod boots clashing on the floor. Without discussion or even consideration, the long-time companions placed themselves back to back, a sword's length apart, as they surveyed their new surroundings.

The Dane moved with a catlike grace that belied his bulk. He slipped from his belt the bearded axe he favored; Cormac drew his long sword.

"Where *is* this place?" Wulfhere demanded peevishly.

Above them arched a dome three hundred feet in diameter, gold or gold-plated unless the eerie light tricked Cormac's eyes. The dome rested on sixteen massive pillars, arranged in pairs. The shafts were of red-veined yellow marble with sharp-edged fluting of the Doric order, but the bases and capitals were ornate and apparently solid silver.

The dome was at one end of a rectangular building six hundred feet long. The remainder of the structure formed a pillared courtyard, an anteroom to the domed sanctum of what was clearly a temple. Nothing moved but the whispering breeze.

Cormac glanced again at the floor set with stone hexagons three feet across their parallel flats. The veined yellow marble formed roseate patterns with slabs of black and with pure white slabs, though the bilious light stained the latter to its own hue. The

blocks were bedded into place with strips of metal—
not lead, but rather gold so pure that it was as soft
and pliable as lead.

The huge structure had an aura of age as uncanny
as the evil light which bathed it.

"*What is this place?*" Wulfhere shouted. His voice
woke echoes from the pillars and then, a half-second
delayed, from the dome above them.

A crowd of men and women poured in through the
temple's front entrance, chittering to one another.
The folk had brown complexions and were so short
that Cormac's first thought was of a tribe of monkeys
playing in ancient ruins.

There were nearly a hundred of them. They wore
clothing so dull and shapeless that it required a
moment's consideration to be certain it was of woven
fabric rather than the pelts of beasts.

Cormac's shield, a small buckler, was strapped to
his back. He tugged it free, settling the paired handles
into his left fist. The iron boss and rim themselves
were useful weapons, though none of this crowd
appeared to be armed.

"Keep away!" Wulfhere shouted over his left shoulder to the little strangers.

The Dane was poised with his axe lifted in both
hands. The blade's hooked lower edge could drag a
horseman from his mount or pull an opponent's shield
clear for a quick upward thrust to finish a battle. As
a threat against these brown strangers, the weapon
looked as out of place as it would have been in a
sheepfold.

The little folk spilled around Cormac and Wulfhere.
Their voices were as constant and meaningless as the
buzz of bees. The tallest of the folk barely rose to the
height of Cormac's armpit. They fingered the reivers'
clothing and accoutrements, pressing close in wonder
but never making eye contact.

Wulfhere shouted a great curse. He raised his foot

and thrust out, not so much kicking as pushing off the most insistent of the folk who tugged at his dagger sheath. The little man—or perhaps a woman—skidded across the floor, squealing in terror. The whole crowd darted back with the suddenness of a flock of pigeons changing course.

A door at the back of the building opened. Cormac had missed the hinged panel in the coffering which ornamented all the walls. Through the doorway stepped a man in a purple robe with gold lace at the throat and hem. He was black-haired and of normal height, though nowhere near the size of the armored warriors.

The newcomer raised his hand and called to the stunted folk in a liquid version of what was obviously the language that they chirped among themselves. The crowd bobbed to the floor in abasement, then dispersed through the front door and pillared side aisles. A dozen or so remained beneath the dome, waiting for further direction.

"Peace be on you, strangers," the man called in rough-hewn but intelligible Gaelic. "I am Creon, the—king, I suppose you would say, of this accursed isle. And this—"

Creon didn't look around, but through the doorway behind him stepped another figure: a woman, younger and dressed in white with gold trim. Her features, like her pale complexion and black hair, were similar to those of the man; but whereas Creon was merely handsome, the woman was startlingly beautiful.

"—is my daughter Antheia," Creon finished, smiling slightly to notice the reivers staring with interest and appraisal toward the woman.

"What *is* this place?" Cormac called, echoing Wulfhere's demand of moments before.

"This place . . ." said Antheia. Her voice had a bell-like clarity, and the Gaelic rolled from her tongue without Creon's stilted choppiness. ". . . is all that remains of fabled Atlantis."

"You speak Gaelic," Wulfhere said accusingly. He lowered his axe only to high port, slanted across his chest; one hand on the end of the helve, the other gripping just beneath the broad blade. Cormac knew that his friend could lop Creon and his daughter into halves with a single stroke; and he knew also that Wulfhere was extremely dangerous when, as now, he was confused.

"Yes," Antheia said in German so distorted that it was a moment before the words fell into Cormac's mental template. "And we learned the speech of Saxon castaways also. Though not—" she added with a smile when she saw the reivers' puzzled expressions "—very well, I gather."

A bustle at the temple's distant entrance spun Wulfhere. He lifted his axe for a blow that could crush through an elephant's armor. Some of the stunted folk were back now, bringing wicker trays covered with fruits, nuts and berries.

The Dane lowered his axe in embarrassment, then thrust the helve back under his belt. Cormac smiled faintly and sheathed his sword. He'd want to dry the scabbard, wipe and oil the blade . . . but in good time, not just now.

"You are Atlanteans, then?" he asked.

Creon smiled without humor. "*They* are Atlanteans," he said, gesturing toward the brown servants bringing in the trays of viands. "My daughter and I are the last descendants of the Athenians who conquered the island in the moments before its collapse into the sea."

Creon crossed his arms and swept his grim gaze around the temple and the folk within it. "We Greeks decayed in numbers," he said. "*They* decayed in stature and intelligence—in the arts and in everything that raises humanity from the beasts. The end must be very soon for the Atlanteans and us, their masters, alike."

"Where *are* we?" Wulfhere demanded in a snarl of frustration. He strode toward the pillared side-aisle, moving with a speed and grace that belied the notion that a man the Dane's size must be clumsy.

A brown-skinned woman offered Wulfhere ripe pears. He danced around her. There was no contact, but the Atlantean dropped her tray in terror and hid her face in her hands.

Cormac slid by instinct to Wulfhere's left side as he left the nave, ready to cover the Dane if an axe-stroke drew the bigger man off-balance. They had survived, the two of them, because they fought as a team rather than as two individuals. A hundred times each had blocked the side-thrust spear from his friend's armpit or the sword swung at the back of the other's helmet.

At the moment, no armed foe threatened Cormac and Wulfhere in this place, this Atlantis; but the Gael had known evil enough in his wanderings to feel its presence here.

They stepped out onto the edge of the slab which leveled the temple's foundations. A paved court had once surrounded the building, but grass and even mighty trees now shouldered aside the blocks of hexagonal marble.

A rectangular building clad in tin or tarnished silver faced the temple. The expanse of courtyard between the buildings had been kept clear of vegetation. The silver structure was two stories high and of considerable size, though it was by no means comparable to the domed temple. Atlantean servants with trays scuttled from there to the temple. They halted nervously when they noticed Cormac and Wulfhere watching them.

Antheia came out beside the reivers. Cormac

couldn't read the hint of a smile she gave him. He noticed for the first time that Antheia's robe was clasped at the left shoulder by a brilliant ruby. That stone and the similar jewel which her father wore were the only objects in this *place* which seemed unaffected by the sickly light.

The thought drew Cormac's gaze upward. He squinted, holding the back of his left hand across his eyes so that the fingers formed slitted protection.

He'd expected the sun, however distorted or cruelly-filtered its beams might be. Instead, a ball of purple-green light hung only a moderate distance— miles or at most tens of miles—above the temple's dome. The ball had a measurable diameter rather than being a dazzling point like the true sun.

Swirls of sickly color paraded across the sphere's displayed surface. Its glow provided the sole illumination of the world below.

Cormac lowered his eyes, shivering despite himself. Until he saw *that*, he hadn't truly believed that something had snatched him from his former reality. Wherever Atlantis was, it was not in a place or time that Cormac's world knew.

"How did we get here, girl?" Wulfhere asked in a soft voice. Only someone who knew the Dane as well as Cormac did would have realized that Wulfhere was on the edge of berserk fury.

"Sometimes the bubble in which we all are trapped draws things from outside itself," Antheia replied. She spoke calmly, but a tic in the corner of her eye suggested she read Wulfhere's mood better than the Gael had feared she would. "Driftwood, seabirds . . . Men, not often, but often enough in the millennia since the bulk of the island sank."

"In my day and that of my daughter," said Creon, who joined them from between two of the close-set columns, "there have been Christian monks from

Ireland and pirates who call themselves Saxons and Jutes. And yourselves, good sirs."

He nodded with sad finality.

An animal hooted in pain or triumph from the near distance. The sound was the first sign that anything existed beyond the ruins fringing the overgrown courtyard.

"How do we get out of here, then?" Cormac demanded. His voice didn't rise after the second syllable, but that was only because he consciously suppressed the spike of terror. "How do we return to the world we came from?"

Though that world was a storm-tossed sea ready to swallow the reivers within minutes or less . . .

"No one has left Atlantis in ten millennia," Creon said. "None of my ancestors succeeded, none of the later castaways. We are all trapped."

"Though there are worse worlds to be trapped in," his daughter added with a speculative look at Cormac. "Especially now."

The Gael was in no mood for a woman, even a woman as lovely as Antheia. He eyed the pillar behind him.

The temple's outer columns were massive constructions in their own right, though they were nowhere near the size of the eight pairs which directly supported the dome. The shafts were about four feet in diameter, wider than a man could encircle with his arms.

The columns had been assembled from stone barrels as thick as they were wide. The cylinders were rolled onto the site with relative ease, then fluted and polished when transport was complete.

When the columns were first erected, the joints between the barrels may have been so close as to be invisible from all but the most careful examination. However, even if the atmosphere of Atlantis were always as still as this silent, muggy present, it decayed the stone to a degree.

Over the ten thousand years Creon claimed—and surely it could not have been *so* long? But over however many years, cracks that originally wouldn't pass a knifeblade were etched away into ledges for Cormac's fingers and toeholds for his boots. He began to climb as he had often climbed the friable rock of a sea cliff, preparing to take a coast watcher unaware.

Below him, Cormac heard the Dane say, "These others, then—where are they? I don't care about your monks, but if there are Saxons, they are no friends to me.

"The last monk died a year ago," Antheia responded. "Cearbhall, his name was. He was an old man, and never well since the storm which carried him to us, to here."

She didn't speak loudly, but her voice carried over the skritch of Cormac's boots as he mounted from handhold to foothold. The Gael took no risks: three of his limbs were always anchored when he raised the fourth to its new position.

The surroundings of the temple opened out into a verdant jungle. Greenery was occasionally punctuated by a gleaming metal roof or, more often, by a lonely wall which was all that survived of a building.

"The Saxons were men of action, as you gentlemen are," Creon said. "Though I hope their example will prevent you from seeking the same doom. The ground on which we stand is an island. It's surrounded by a belt of water—a moat, you could almost say. Before the collapse, the island was joined to a pair of encircling ring islands and to the mainland beyond by bridges, but those were thrown down by earthquakes when most of the continent sank."

A fig tree grew out of the side of the column forty feet in the air. Seven thumb-thick stems sprouted from where a bird had picked apart the fruit and left pulp containing a seed.

The roots were anchored deep within the column, wedging thousands of tons of stone apart by hydrostatic pressure. Fig wood wasn't especially strong, but the green stems would at worst give warning before they started to crack. Cormac let the plant take enough of his weight that he could survey the horizon.

"Only the innermost of the ring islands was preserved with the temple when the continent sank," Antheia said. "All that remains of Atlantis—all that there is of this world—ends on that island. But Aslief and his Saxons wouldn't believe that, and they died trying to reach what would have been an impenetrable barrier anyway."

Cormac could see a broad belt of water half a mile from where the temple rose. A fish jumped in it. There was nothing unusual about its mackerel-like shape or silvery scales; but unless the angle was deceptive, the fish was ten or a dozen feet in length.

The water belt's unnaturally smooth margins were perfectly circular except where a stand of willows broke the marble coping. The land across the water was similar to that of the central island, though there were fewer visible signs of ruined buildings. Either the earthquake's destruction had been more extensive toward the boundaries of the preserved portion of the continent, or the structures had been less gigantic to begin with.

The further edge of the ring island blurred into purple-green haze, as though the light of the false sun above had been compressed into a membrane. The transition didn't look impenetrable, but there was little to be told from miles' distance in any event.

He and Wulfhere would build a raft—or a true boat, if the Greeks could provide better tools than Cormac's sword and the Dane's war axe. With that and oars or a pole, they would cross to the ring island.

A quick tramp through the undergrowth would bring them to the boundary; and one way or another they would find a way through, though it were a wall of solid steel that they faced when they got there. . . .

"The Saxons built a raft," Creon said. "We warned them of monsters in the water, but they would go anyway. Aslief said they feared not men nor devils, so long as they had their swords in their hands."

"This Aslief," Wulfhere asked. "Was he a man of my height or lacking little of it? The fellow I'm thinking of has blond hair and a silver-mounted spear with a blade broad as a shovel's."

"You've described him to the life," said Antheia. "Aslief Gorm's Bane, he called himself when first he appeared with his men. Was he a friend of yours, sir?"

"No," said Wulfhere without inflection. "But Gorm was my sister's son. I little thought to meet his slayer here."

"Nor shall you," Creon objected. "Aslief and his men built a raft, as I said; and the monsters had their way with them."

Three gigantic fish leaped in unison as close as that of veterans forming the shield wall. Cormac wondered what the creatures lived on. Though the belt of water was half a mile broad and several miles in length . . . If it was as deep as it looked, the volume could support an enormous and varied culture.

"Do you take me for a fool or a townsman?" Wulfhere demanded harshly. "What sort of monster threatens a shipload of Vikings?"

"A monster that rises beneath a raft," Antheia said. Her thin voice suggested her nostrils had tightened with anger at being called by implication a liar. "A monster that plucks the limbs from men as they try to swim to safety. A monster which leaves the bodies of those who sink for the squids with armored shells, which would be danger enough."

Where the giant fish had leaped a moment before,

a fifty-foot shadow rose to the surface. The head made Cormac think of a smooth-skinned crocodile, but crocs were neckless. This creature had a neck half the enormous length of its head.

The body was barrel-shaped and powerful. Instead of legs it had flippers which, as the Gael watched, rotated like a seabird's wings for another stroke. The creature drove forward at speed remarkable in something so large. Its hide was black and shiny; conical teeth to cut as well as pierce filled the long jaws.

Another age would call the creature a kronosaur. Cormac had no word for it, but *sea monster* was both accurate and evocative.

The kronosaur submerged with no more commotion than an arrow makes slicing the water. No sign of the creature remained on the surface, though waves of its swift underwater passage buffeted the margins of the land.

As the monster dived, Cormac caught a glimpse of movement on the shore of the ring island. It could have been a goat rising on hind legs to nibble leaves, or even a trick of light and breeze which fluttered the pale undersurface of foliage into the semblance of a human figure. The distance was too far for certainty.

Cormac was certain nonetheless: there were men across the haunted water. He started down, moving with the same easy caution as he had mounted to the vantage point.

The view had given him information, but that opened more questions than it answered. The only thing of which Cormac Mac Art was certain was that he had to get out of this place—though escape meant drowning in the clean salt seas of his own world.

Perhaps the color of the light here made him uneasy. There was nothing else to justify the loathing he felt.

"Who did this, then?" Wulfhere demanded. "Who

cut this place off and left it as a trap for decent seamen?"

The Dane's great fingers played with his axe, lifting it a few inches and then slapping it down against the supporting belt. If his agitation continued to build, he was likely to slide the weapon free and begin making passes that were the last prelude to berserk rage.

If frustration drove Wulfhere berserk without an obvious enemy, well . . . the Dane would find an enemy.

"The continent of Atlantis had been raised from the sea by the might of its wizards," Creon said. "The land was always unstable. The Atlanteans turned their wizardry against us—against our Athenian ancestors when our fleet approached. When we broke through their defenses, the whole system began to collapse. Only enough of the power remained to save the very citadel—this island, and the first of the rings surrounding it."

Cormac dropped to the stone beside the Greeks and Wulfhere. Brown-skinned servants watched from the interior of the temple, but none of them came out to join their rulers.

"There's men across the water!" Cormac said cheerfully, clasping his friend enthusiastically by the shoulders. He had to deflect Wulfhere from the path his mind was treading or they'd none of them be safe. "People, at any rate—women as well as men, I suppose."

He fixed Creon with hard eyes. "That's correct, isn't it? There *are* people on the outer island?"

"Yes, certainly," Creon agreed without hesitation. "Some scores, perhaps hundreds of Atlanteans. They're taller and straighter than their relatives here—"

He gestured dismissively toward the servants waiting within the aisle of the temple.

"—but they've sunk even deeper into savagery. They live like beasts."

Cormac gave Wulfhere a friendly shake and released him. The Dane would be all right now. The trouble with Wulfhere was that in a doubtful situation, he always turned to his axe for succor. In the bloody age left by Rome's collapse, Wulfhere's instinct for slaughter had proved a major survival trait, but here it could cause problems.

"We're fortunate that the water provides a barrier," Antheia added coolly. "Otherwise they would have slaughtered us long since. And probably have killed their own kin, too. Mere animals."

Cormac looked at the woman. "If the Atlanteans were such great magicians . . ." he said. His tones rasped like steel on a whetstone. "How is it you could crush them to their present state?"

"Because," Antheia responded with a smile as shimmering and hard as a sword edge, "we were greater magicians yet. And before you ask—I have no Atlantean blood myself. Some of the greatest Athenian wizards were women, and one of them reached the citadel before the collapse."

Wulfhere shook himself like a a bear drying its fur in the shelter of a cave. His eyes were bright, but they had lost the glaze of madness which had begun to shutter them.

"I want food," he said in a deep rumble. "And I don't mean muck like what those midgets were offering us. I want meat!"

Creon smiled. "Yes," he said. "I asked the servants to begin boiling a goat as soon as you arrived. We'll go to the palace now."

Antheia laughed and laid the tips of her slim fingers on Cormac's armored shoulder. "And if one goat isn't enough," she said, leading the Gael toward the front door of the temple as though her touch was a leash, "then we will cook more until you're satisfied. After that we can consider your other appetites, not so?"

Her laughter was birdsong in shadowed jungle.

The palace was the metal-clad building facing the temple. Antheia led the way there with her hand resting lightly on Cormac's arm. She talked not of the present but of the Atlantis that once had been, of the time when the island on which they stood was only the governmental complex controlling a continent. The city proper was built on the mainland beyond the ring island—lost for thousands of years beneath the storm-tossed seas.

The Gael looked over his shoulder when they were midway between palace and temple. The latter actually looked larger from the outside than it had when he was within. A pediment bright with statues of unblemished gold glared down, supported on four sweeping pillars. Though the peak was only half as high as the curve of the dome, it gave the impression of looming upward.

The temple's interior closed in on itself. Creon and Antheia had come from the vaults under the nave to greet the reivers. Cormac wondered what lay there.

The palace looked increasingly run-down as they drew closer. The silver had been applied in finger-thick slabs rather than mere foil over the stone, but many plates hung skewed from their rivets or had fallen away completely. Though the surfaces were black with oxide, they still reflected the sickly light of the false sun.

"Doesn't that thing ever set?" Cormac demanded harshly. The shock of anger he felt as he spoke warned him that his nerves were nearly as close to the edge as Wulfhere's.

"It will burn so long as this world remains," Antheia said. "The highest wizards of Atlantis created this place to be their final refuge, the den in which they could survive though all the continent else were conquered by an enemy."

She showed Cormac a smile as bitter as that of a victim for her executioner. "They didn't expect that we would penetrate their sanctum so swiftly and displace them," she said. "But on the other hand, we— my ancestors—didn't expect to be trapped here forevermore."

She hugged herself close to the Gael, as though she were unaware of his salt-crusted armor and his lack of response. "We have lamps within the palace," she said. "We'll shutter the windows while we eat. And afterwards—"

Antheia gave a throaty chuckle. "Afterwards, there's no need of light at all, unless you want one."

Under other circumstances, Wulfhere might have complained that the goat wasn't well enough done— and in all truth, it was scarcely cooked at all. The long-ship had been tossed for a day and a half, giving the crew no opportunity to eat more than mouthfuls of hard bread washed down with ale heavily salted by the spray.

Hunger conquered the Dane's normal insistence on meat boiled till it fell off the bones. He wolfed down chunks of the dark, grainy goat, tearing it away with his strong teeth. The servants provided wine and, when the Dane asked for it, mead with a musty, powerful kick that he drank with still greater gusto.

Wulfhere was relaxing, though he still wore his iron corselet. He hung his axe from the top of the table beside him without consideration for the scar its hook put in the ivory inlays. Creon and Antheia didn't appear to notice.

The four of them sat on backless stools of bronze cast in a filigree. The furniture was draped with wool dyed muddy purple. The fabric was obviously of more recent manufacture than the metalwork.

Cormac looked around. A thought had frozen his jaws midway through a morsel of shoulder muscle more red than pink. Atlantis was a display of human progress, from the magnificent past to a present of near-bestial savagery. And wasn't this a description of the outer world as well, where Rome's collapse had loosed on the seas creatures like—

Creatures like Cormac Mac Art.

Cormac gave a choking snarl of a laugh. *He* hadn't made the world. If Mankind's natural state was barbarism—so be it. And so much the worse for soft folk who lacked Cormac's strength, his speed, and his absolute willingness to die so long as he was able to kill . . .

The two Greeks stared at him. He'd drawn their eyes when he laughed, though they might not have realized the sound *was* laughter. Wulfhere slammed down an agate cup for the servant with the sack of mead to refill—again. He fished a gobbet of meat from the pot with his dagger.

"Just thinking about how we were going to get out of here," Cormac lied to the Greeks.

"You bet we are," the Dane muttered. If he'd waited for an Atlantean to serve him, the meat would have been sliced into at least a dozen bites before it was transferred to Wulfhere's plate. "But first we're going to have a little something to eat . . ."

The walls of the dining room were covered in brass with low reliefs depicting planting and harvest. Reed torches, their pith soaked in oil, burned in free-standing sconces of delicate bronze. The wavering rushlights emphasized the artistry of the ancient furnishings.

The ceiling had painted decorations within the coffers, but these were by now no more than shadows. The soot of millennia caked them. That brought home to Cormac the age of this place better than did the deteriorated stone of the temple.

Cormac reached for his wine cup, a broad goblet

of silver-mounted rock crystal. Only lees remained in
it. Before a servant could act, Antheia took the footed
bowl herself and filled the cup with unmixed wine.
The local vintage was raw, but its alcohol content was
higher than that of any wine which Cormac had
drunk before.

Perhaps something about the light affected the
vines, or it might be that the fermenting culture was
an ancient one.

"Are you becoming—satisfied?" Antheia asked
coquettishly, apparently oblivious of her father across
the round table. She had doffed her outer robe for
dinner. The inner tunic was white also and diapha-
nous. Antheia wore a girdle and bandeau of metal
network, confining but not in the least concealing her
breasts and hips.

The ruby brooch, pinned now to the shoulder of
the tunic, glowed with an internal fire which owed
nothing to the quivering torches. The bezel was of
untarnished electrum, cast in the shape of a serpent
swallowing its own tail. Cormac looked at the stone,
wondering how much of the ancient wizards' magic
remained under the control of their descendants.

Antheia's breasts were small but full enough to sag
slightly within the mesh bandeau. She deliberately
brushed her bosom across Cormac's eyes as he stared
at the ruby. The fabric of her tunic was slick as glass,
and her nipples were erect.

"So you're only interested in my jewelry?" she
gibed, straightening away from the Gael. "And I took
you for a man!"

Wulfhere flung a rack of rib bones under the table,
then slurped his mead bowl empty. The floor was of
stone hexagons like those of the temple, though these
were all of the yellow marble. The masons had set
them so that the red veins matched from slab to slab,
with only the metal edging to break the pattern.

There were no hounds under the table to devour

the Dane's leavings. Cormac supposed the servants would clean up after the guests left the room. Creon, nibbling on fruit throughout the meal, smiled indulgently at the Dane. If he noticed his daughter's interest in Cormac—and he could scarcely not have noticed—then he was complaisant regarding her behavior.

Not that the slim Greek could stop the reivers from doing anything they pleased. . . .

Cormac looked at Antheia. She smiled and tossed her head. A golden net gathered the hair at the base of her skull, but beneath that the black strands fell free to her supple waist.

He was fed and rested and out of the sickly glare of the false sun. Antheia did please him. She would have pleased a monk vowed to celibacy.

Cormac lurched to his feet. The wine had even more of a bite than he'd realized, but he'd never in his life drunk so much that he couldn't prove himself a man in whatever terms the arena required.

Antheia slipped a rushlight from its sconce. Her smile was enchantment itself. "Come," she said. "There are some remains of the old magic in my apartment that will amuse you."

Wulfhere set down his empty goblet. The servant bent to it. The Dane gave a rumbling belch that startled the little Atlantean away with a squeal.

"Be well, my daughter," Creon said. "I'll endeavor to entertain our other guest while you're gone."

Cormac followed the woman into a hallway which once had been paneled with ivory and rare woods. The organic materials had rotted to dust, leaving only the frames of precious metals clinging to the stone core. Servants peered nervously from alcoves.

Twenty yards down the corridor, Antheia opened a door and motioned Cormac inside before shutting it behind them. There was a latch but no lock. The panel was leather-covered wood. Curlicues of brass nails studded it in an attempt at decoration. The Gael could have punched his fist through the door.

Antheia thrust her torch into a sconce shaped like an open-mouthed dragon. The room's other furnishings consisted of a bronze bench and number of metalwork chests against the walls. A circular bed was visible through the open doorway to an inner room.

Cormac reached for the woman. She eeled through his arms, caught his right hand and pressed it to her breast, and was out of reach again before he could turn the touch into a grip.

"Take that nasty armor off," Antheia commanded lightly as she opened one of the chests. The container was almost as tall as she was, but it was no more than a foot through or across.

"It won't get in the way," Cormac rumbled thickly. "The first time, at any rate."

He started for the woman. She giggled. Trails of blue light, wavering like threads being spun into a skein, lifted from the top of the device as she fingered it.

"See?" Antheia said. "Ancient magic, as I told you. Touch it—it feels good."

The light wobbled slowly from the chest and began to extend vaguely in the direction of Cormac and the door.

"Turn that off," Cormac said.

He was rapidly becoming sober again. His shoulders hit stone, startling him to the edge of white rage before he realized that he'd backed against the wall. He hadn't thought he'd moved so far away . . .

Silvery horns a few inches long rotated on the top of the chest, emitting blue light the way a spider's spinnerets ooze silk. Antheia's fingers danced on a metal pad behind the horns. Her eyes were on Cormac rather than the controls she manipulated. The skein of blue continued to expand, but it no longer snuffled toward the Gael.

"Silly, it's harmless," the woman laughed. "Watch me."

There was commotion down the hall, metal banging on stone. A bench had overturned.

"Wulfhere?" Cormac called. His right hand hovered near the pommel of his sword. Embarrassment prevented him from drawing the weapon. He didn't have a good reason for being so afraid.

Antheia, one slim hand still on the controls of the device, stepped fully into the blue light. The pattern flowed past and around her like water pouring over a glass statue. The jewel on her shoulder blazed with redoubled fury, taking no color from the skein through which it glared.

A sheen, vaguely purple and as thin as isinglass, lay on the woman's skin and garments. The hue tinged both the portion within the blue light, and her legs from the thighs down which were below the skein.

"See?" Antheia said. "Harmless."

Her voice bubbled as though she were speaking from underwater. She held her free hand out to Cormac enticingly. The blue threads lurched in his direction again.

"Stop—" Cormac shouted. His sword sang from its scabbard. "—that, or—"

The suite's flimsy door burst inward. A brown-skinned man with the muscular body of an athlete lunged through the opening. He wore a beaded breechclout, a headband, and a torque of copper strips. His stone-headed axe was already swinging down in a mighty cast as the door flew out of his way.

Cormac stabbed the warrior sideways through the rib cage. The fellow didn't realize the Gael was present until the sword sliced his lungs and took the two lower chambers off his heart. The savage tried to cry out, but his surprise drowned in a spray of blood from his mouth and nostrils.

There were ten or a dozen warriors in the corridor

behind the first victim, pressing forward and carrying the corpse with them as Cormac tried to clear his sword. Steel shrieked against bone as he dragged the blade back.

The skein of blue light enveloped Antheia wholly. Her visage was harsh and desperate. The first savage's axe hung at the edge of the blue cocoon. The weapon sank slowly toward the floor, as if it had fallen into a vat of cold treacle.

Cormac fumbled with his left hand, trying to find the buckler which ought to hang behind his hip. The shield was in the dining room where he'd left it.

A spear slammed Cormac full in the chest. His mail was of double-wound links riveted for strength. It held, but the blow rocked him bruisingly. His attackers might be the same race as the Atlantean servants, but there was nothing physically degenerate about them.

Cormac jumped back, finally freeing his weapon. He swung clumsily but with desperate speed to block the blade of a savage slashing at his face. The other sword was bronze, cast in the attractive curves of a poplar leaf. Cormac's steel—a long Roman cavalry weapon, forged in Bilbao—sheared the bronze where it narrowed near the grip, then clopped into the savage's unprotected skull.

The man went down like a toppling statue. His headband fluttered behind him. Its severed ends were bloody.

The spearman thrust for Cormac again. This time the Gael was ready for him. The spearshaft was wrist-thick cornelwood, too sturdy to sever confidently with a swordblade. Cormac instead used the shaft itself as a chopping block to lop off the savage's leading hand. The spearpoint wavered aside without the left hand to guide it. Cormac back-slashed through the savage's throat, choking his scream into a gurgle.

Cormac drew the dagger from his belt and waded

into his opponents at close quarters. These Atlantean savages were sturdy men, but they were naked and none of them was near the Gael's size.

The blade of the Spanish dagger was five fingers broad at the hilt. Cormac ripped the edge up through cartilage where ribs joined the breastbone. He used the dying victim as a shield while his sword struck right and left above the limp shoulders. Two more savages fell, hacked so fiercely that Cormac's steel split their collarbones and severed the great blood vessels rising from the heart.

A bronze warhammer smashed into Cormac's side. The Atlantean was squat and powerful. He'd swung the weapon with both arms and the full strength of his body. Despite the mail and its quilted leather backing, the impact shot dazzling pain through Cormac's ribs. It numbed his side for an instant.

The savage had been pulled off-balance by his own blow. He stumbled forward as he tried to follow up the shocking impact. Before he could recover, the Gael's dagger took him at the base of the jaw, thrusting upward like a gaff through the gills of a struggling trout. The body went into spastic convulsions as Cormac flung it aside.

The surviving savages broke and ran. Metal clanged as they tripped on fallen equipment. Some of them flung weapons away to speed their flight.

Cormac staggered after them. He ignored Antheia; she remained in her wrap of clinging light. The stone axe had finally reached the floor. A spear, caught in the same ambiance, was sinking slowly after the axe.

There was a stitch in Cormac's side from the hammerblow, and pain blurred his vision every time his right heel hit the floor. The tip of the Gael's sword ripped red sparks along the stones at eye height; weakness from the injury had caused him to drift closer to the wall than he had understood. He cursed and brought his mind back in focus by an effort of will.

If the tip of a broken rib had pierced his lung, he would know it by now from the bloody froth he'd be exhaling. *That* hadn't happened, and anything else was mere pain.

Pain was nothing at all when Wulfhere was at risk and there were enemies to kill.

The servants had disappeared. The last of the attacking savages darted into the dining room. The Gael followed, thrusting the fleeing man through the small of the back.

The dining room was chaos. Two rushlights remained, but most of the illumination now came from a skein of glowing threads like those which had wavered toward Cormac in the moments before the savages attacked.

Creon stood within a ball of blue light emanating from another vertical chest. Instead of manipulating the control panel, the Greek gestured. Pseudopods of fibrous light extended in the directions he stretched his arms. The threads gripped the throats of two savages, lifting their bodies off the floor as it throttled them.

More than a score of other savages crowded the room, stabbing and hacking at the envelope of light. A number of the attackers were women. An age-frail man held out a wand that could, in the doubtful illumination, have been either crystal or metal. Instead of a cloth headband, he wore a cap of spiral mesh formed from wires of gold, silver, and their alloy electrum.

A hexagonal block had been displaced from the flooring. As Cormac entered the room, he saw Wulfhere's bound legs disappearing into the hole beneath where the slab had been.

Cormac hit the savages as a scythe does a wheatfield. There was no time for finesse: numbers would bear him down if his foes had an instant to organize against the fresh danger. The Roman sword whirled in wide arcs. When a savage ducked close, Cormac disemboweled him with a hooking cut of the dagger.

A sword's point is the trained killer's tool. The edge is spectacular but far less lethal in its effects. Cormac knew that well, but at this juncture he slashed nonetheless instead of thrusting deep for each opponent's life.

A well-placed thrust lets a man's life out in a minute or so when his heart has pumped the blood-vessels empty. During that minute, the victim is as deadly an opponent as before he got his death wound.

What Cormac required to survive this maelstrom was terror and disablement. An eight-inch gouge along a rib cage spread like the jaws of Hell when tensioning muscles drew the edges of the skin apart. The wound wasn't as dangerous as a heart thrust, but the shock of it stunned the victim and terrified his friends.

A hand severed at the wrist could no longer hold an axe. A head wound need not penetrate the skull to bludgeon the victim into dazed helplessness.

The chieftain with the wand shouted an order. Surviving savages scrambled down the hole in the flooring. Cormac's attack had been so sudden and overwhelming that there was no real attempt to withstand him. Warriors, some of them women, flung up weapons for self-protection, but in the dim-lit chaos they didn't realize their assailant was alone and therefore vulnerable.

Cormac was in a killing rage. He didn't care if his foes ran or stood. The Gael sheared the spine of a fleeing savage, then swung at the chieftain who raised the wand against him.

The tip of the wand spun tendrils of blue fire like those emanating from the Greeks' devices. Light caught the blade, slowed it, and finally froze the sword in mid-air.

"May the pigs eat your flesh!" Cormac screamed as he pressed close and stabbed upward with his dagger.

The chieftain dodged back. More tendrils whirled from the wand tip and wrapped the Gael's left wrist. Their touch was cold as a drowned corpse.

Behind the chieftain, the last of his whole-bodied followers dived into the hole. The savage tugged on the hexagon he and his fellows had displaced to launch their attack. The stone toppled into the hole sideways and stuck, wedged by its great weight against the sides of the cavity.

Crippled victims of the Gael's attack screamed and groped on the floor, blind from head wounds and fear. Creon continued to hold the pair his device had captured. The Greek's face looked as strained as that of a man being crucified.

Cormac forced his body toward the chieftain. His sword and left hand were held as firmly as if gyred to the living rock. A separate tendril flicked down to wrap his right wrist lest he drop the sword and strike his opponent with his clenched fist.

Antheia entered the room, carrying a sword from one of the savages. A handful of the stunted servants followed her.

"Father!" she cried. She had aged decades since Cormac last saw her.

The Atlantean chieftain spun away. Blue fibers released Cormac from their grip. The chieftain hurled his wand toward the hole. It struck the skewed block and clattered down to the savages below.

The chieftain was toppling forward. Cormac's sword tore deeply through his back and spine, but the Roman steel was slicing a man already dead.

The volume of light encircling Creon sucked inward with the abruptness of a bubble bursting. The Greek staggered, scarcely able to keep his feet when the strain of his activity was released.

"They got through the tunnels," he gasped to his daughter. "Despite the Guardian. They had a wand of power."

Creon looked . . . old, *ancient*. Cormac was reminded of the withered features of the chieftain as the two of them struggled breast to breast.

The Gael stripped the breechclout from a corpse. The garment was made of leather, sliced thin and sueded. Clamshells individually smaller than a fingernail were stitched hollow-side out in a pattern, alternating blue nacre with yellow.

Cormac wiped his sword, then his dagger, with the breechclout. He inhaled in racking gasps. He had to bring his quivering muscles and his breathing under control before he attempted the next stage of what was necessary.

The room's walls and ceiling were splotched with traceries of blood slung from the Gael's swordpoint. Most of a man's wadded scalp stuck over the lintel. The floor looked flat, but thousands of years of footsteps had worn troughs in the stone. Blood pooled there, as much as an inch deep.

"A wand of power?" Antheia repeated. "After so long? That's impossible!"

"No, but the drain is terrible," Creon replied. "Look, this is the one who was using it."

He touched the corpse of the chieftain with the toe of his sandal. The forearm of the corpse crumbled. The flesh was as dry and flaky as if it had baked for a year in desert sunlight.

"Where," said Cormac, "is Wulfhere?"

His chest still pumped vast amounts of air through his open mouth, but his breathing had settled into a regular pattern instead of the desperation of a man saved from drowning. Cormac didn't have his full strength back, but the spasms that had followed his adrenaline-fueled exertions had passed.

He wasn't in perfect condition; but life wasn't perfect, and the present situation was *far* less than perfect. His body would serve.

The Greeks stared at him.

"The Atlanteans took your friend with them," Creon said. "Tribesmen from the ring, attacking through the tunnels beneath the moat. I can't imagine what they wanted with him. They can't have known anyone was present but Antheia and I."

The Greek looked at his daughter and added, "I captured two of them. Did you . . . ?"

She shook her head sharply. "No," she said, "no. Are any of these suitable for use?"

She glanced around the carnage the Gael had left of the raiding party. Lopped limbs, coils of intestines tangling the feet of a victim who had tried to run despite his wound; a woman who lay limp in a roundel of blood, her glassy eyes staring upward . . .

"No," Antheia said. "I see."

"Where did they take him?" Cormac repeated in a voice so loud that the words battered the walls like fists.

"How—" Antheia said; and froze, seeing her death at the end of the hot reply. She had aged horribly. The price of the power she and her father wielded was nearly as high as that of the wand Cormac watched kill its user.

"I suppose they would have taken him to wherever they live on the ring island," Creon said. "If the Guardian doesn't get them all, despite the wand. I wouldn't believe they could make it past him, had they not done so."

Creon backed and sagged against the chest from which the light sprang. Cormac poised, but the Greek was only reaching for support. He looked like a scarecrow instead of the vibrant man of middle age who had greeted the castaways.

Cormac had sheathed his dagger after he cleaned it. Now he shot the long sword back in its scabbard and stepped to the hole in the floor. He could glimpse light of sorts past the skewed block, a pale glow too even to come from a lamp.

"You can't go down there!" Antheia protested. "The Guardian is—"

"Unless the savages killed it?" Creon suggested in sudden fear.

Antheia turned on him. "With a single wand?" she snarled. "Don't be a fool. You and I together couldn't manage it, and that was when it was smaller!"

Cormac touched the block of stone, not gripping it but judging the texture and finding places at which he *could* grip.

"You can't go down there," Creon said in shocked anger. "It's—you'd be throwing yourself away, merely feeding the Guardian."

Cormac looked back over his shoulder. The savages whom Creon had choked comatose were on the floor where the device dropped them. Servants bound the captives' wrists and legs with ribbons of raw silk, no less strong for its lustrous beauty.

Bandages of the same material wrapped Wulfhere's ankles as the savages dragged the Dane away.

Cormac straightened in a smooth motion that proved his muscles were under his full control. He raised one of the bronze stools by a leg and shook the draping fabric from it. Creon started back; servants ran squealing in wide-eyed terror.

Antheia's left hand closed on her ruby brooch. Her face was cool and emotionless.

Cormac swung the stool overhead as he would have used a flail. He released the metal an instant before it crashed into the chest from which Creon spun blue light. The Gael didn't want to touch the device, and he didn't want to touch any*thing* that touched the device in the moment of its destruction.

Bronze chest and bronze stool melded in a ringing crash. The metal glowed, not blue but a hot yellow-orange like the core of a charcoal kiln. Molten bronze spattered in all directions with the smell of something foul burning.

The servants had fled. A dying savage moaned softly. The Greeks stood transfixed.

"So you'd treat us as you were doing these folk?" the Gael shouted, gesturing left-handed toward the bound savages. "Choke us, tie us—and then what, I wonder?"

His voice had a musical lilt, as playful as a cat's paw. He spat on Creon's sandaled foot. "Get out of here before I deal with you as I did your evil toy!"

The Greeks swept from the room, silent and blank-faced. A spot on Creon's robe smoldered from a spark thrown out by his melting device.

Cormac squatted and gripped the block of stone. The iron chape of his scabbard skittered on the floor.

Wulfhere's bow and quiver stood in a corner, but the bearded axe had vanished with the Dane. Hope had no more to do with Cormac's actions than fear did, but—

If Wulfhere believed in anything, he believed not in a god or gods but rather in that axe which had cut through every foe he faced. So long as the Dane and his axe were together, woe to their enemies.

Cormac squeezed and lifted. The stone block was twice a man's weight and awkward, with no proper handholds. Gravity and friction on the sides of the hole fought the Gael's strength. Human muscles won the struggle, raising the block with a grating snarl.

Spinning as his knees straightened, letting the stone's inertia carry the weight past him, Cormac rose from the hole. He released his burden at a calculated moment. The great hexagon smashed down on the

welded mass of what had been Creon's device of
power, crushing the ruin flat with a few additional
sputters.

Cormac snatched up his shield, drew his sword, and
dropped feet-first into the tunnel beneath.

The ground—the pavement—was a full eight feet
below the tunnel's brick ceiling. The savages were folk
of moderate height, even though they weren't stunted
like their kin who served the Greeks. Cormac wondered how they'd been able to lift a massive slab so
high above their heads—then remembered the wand.
The price for its power was a high one, but that power
was real.

The tunnel was a drain, choked at its inner end by
silt and rubble swept down on storm waters. The
lower end, leading to a greater cavern beyond, had
been cleared in the immediate past sufficiently to pass
a line of hastening warriors. The dirt was freshly
turned, and a copper-headed mattock stuck in the
wall. Its shaft had broken when the user tried to lever
out a stone which was actually part of the masonry.

Cormac followed his swordpoint from the tunnel.

The light he had seen came from the coat of fungus
which slimed the floor and stone columns of the vast
world that opened before him. The roof, forty—fifty—
sixty feet above the sloping floor, was covered in metal
which repelled the fungus.

Ripples across the ceiling indicated that the metal
had been twisted fiercely at some time in the past;
some of the support pillars had a shaken look. Pumps
sighed like mighty lungs in the unguessed distance.

This underworld had been a vast dockyard in the
time before the fall of Atlantis. Ramps, now dry save
for the fungus, slanted upward from channels to central quays. The sloping surfaces were meant to hold
vessels drawn out of the water. A fleet that could have
required docks of such extent was—

Was beyond present conception, even for a reiver who had travelled as widely as Cormac Mac Art.

There was no sign of the ships. If they had been docked here at the moment of collapse, then millennia had finished the business of destruction. Fungus lay smooth on the ramps, without so much as a mound to indicate where vessels had been berthed in the dim past.

The channels were twenty feet deep, sufficient for ships of greater draft than any which coursed the seas of Cormac's age. The water had vanished, drained or pumped away when magic ripped the citadel from its proper time and space. Cormac wondered at the power which circulated air and water in this trap that held him; but, like the false sun lighting the surface above, it was a matter beyond his immediate interest.

First he would find and free Wulfhere. Then they would escape. Nothing else mattered.

The savages' trail was easy to follow in the disturbed fungus. They'd crossed a channel, then turned outward along the axis of a quay. Weapons and equipment were scattered at the bottom of the channel. The surface was trampled in a broad circle as though there had been a battle.

Cormac thought there were no bodies, until he noticed that a human forearm lay where fungus had been kicked up in a wave. The bones were crushed at both wrist and elbow ends.

The illumination was deceptive. Because the glow was weak and shadowless, Cormac found it hard to judge distances. He thought he saw movement to his right side. He poised with his buckler advanced, but it was only a vertical slash across a pillar's coating. The slanting mark seemed to move when the Gael caught it in the corner of his eye.

Half of a woman's body lay a hundred yards from the mouth of the drainage tunnel. Her torso had been chewed away, but the legs were still joined to the

pelvis. The head had fallen twenty yards further along
the track.

The woman's features were shrunken with age;
milky cataracts closed both eyes. She'd already been
dead or next breath from dead when some creature
devoured her body.

Cormac jogged on, planting his boots squarely to
keep from slipping on the glowing slime. Echoes
passed strangely among the channels and pillared
aisles. The pumps' sighing was overlaid by a quavering
note that might have been either a harmonic or a
completely unconnected sound. Occasionally he felt a
rumble so deep that it seemed bowel-loosening vibration rather than noise.

As the Gael strode forward, he kept an eye out for
signs of whatever had eaten the savage's body. "The
Guardian" Creon and his daughter spoke of, no doubt;
but they had given no description. There were no
tracks in the fungus coating. Was the creature
winged?

Cormac glanced up—and saw, reflected in the
smooth metal ceiling, the pattern that had eluded him
at ground level. Curving ripples marked the fungus,
each a yard long and nested together into a fuzzy line.
He'd assumed they were caused by stress markings in
the quay.

A similar track paralleled the first, five yards farther
from the path the savages had worn. The nests of
arcs faced one another, concave sides to concavities.
Something many-legged and fifteen feet wide had followed the raiders as they returned through the
tunnels.

A human leg lay on the stone where it had dribbled
from jaws that bolted the remainder of the corpse.
The muscles were shrunken with age and more than
age, like those of the chieftain who struggled with
Cormac in the palace. The savages were using the

wand to fend off their pursuer—and the wand was using them up.

Farther along the track were fragments of another body, too shredded to determine even the species had not Cormac known it must be human. Corpses the wand of power had drained would provide little further sustenance.

As he neared the rim of this bubble world, Cormac found increasing evidence of the damage done when Atlantis submerged. Pillars were twisted on their axes. Some remained staggeringly upright only because of the weight of the ceiling sagging upon them. The metal sheathing was buckled in ridges as much as a foot deep, tracing the curve of ancient shockwaves.

Purple-green light swelled in the near distance. A column had collapsed, dragging with it a section of the surface above. Dirt and rubble lay in a broad ramp toward the world above, though its top lay thirty feet below the hole in the ceiling.

The bones of large animals lay in and near the mound of debris. Half-buried and half-crumbling was the skull of an elephant with a curving tusk longer than that of its kin in Cormac's day. The other tusk was broken off short. Beasts from the ring island had stumbled into the pit and been killed by the fall, just as happened regularly in sinkholes in the world beyond Atlantis.

A purple-green blur tinging the pillars far to Cormac's right suggested there were other, similar tears in the cavern's fabric. He couldn't guess at the total, two or three or possibly scores.

But whatever the number of such pitfalls, they provided sufficient food to keep *something* alive for a very long time.

Cormac started up the tumbled ramp, though he didn't know how he would deal with the thirty-foot gap between the top of it and the surface. He didn't have materials for a grapnel. Perhaps he could improvise something with strips of clothing and his dagger. . . .

Clicks, rapid and increasingly loud, came from the glowing vagueness. Echoes hid the direction of approach. Cormac pivoted on his left heel, keeping his buckler close to his body and his swordarm cocked at his side to slash or stab.

A centipede the size of a nightmare curled like a tidal wave over the ramp toward him.

Cormac shouted, thrust out his shield, and whipped his long sword around in an overarm cut. He might as well have slashed at a landslide.

The creature had one feathery antenna and a stump where the other should have been. Its mouth parts were multiple, side-hinged, and hideous. Mandibles dripping a corrosive poison stabbed out, the right glancing along the steel boss of Cormac's buckler as the other thrust toward his chest.

Cormac's sword rang against the centipede's head-shield and rebounded, though the edge left a scar on the chitinous armor. There were other scars, some of them fresh. The blow did nothing to prevent the mandible from striking.

Cormac's mail held, but the ribs beneath were those bruised or cracked during the fight in Antheia's suite. Pain was a white blur that shifted the universe out of focus. Cormac's sword swung again unaffected.

The centipede's eyes were in clumps of six to either side of its armored head. The Gael's steel edge crushed through the lenses of three of the left-hand cluster, splashing clear ichor. The creature's weight rammed Cormac backward off the ramp.

The centipede was a jointed tube, six feet in diameter and longer than the Gael could guess under the circumstances. The legs, one pair to each body segment, splayed out to either side. Their joints sprouted hairs as coarse as tiger whiskers.

Each leg was tipped by a pair of pincers the size

of blacksmith's shears. The creature lifted the front of its body so that the first trio of leg pairs remained free to grip its prey.

Cormac fell on his back. He screamed and chopped sideways with the edge of his shield, clearing two of the pincers fumbling at his mail. The creature's mandibles drew back for another attempt. Behind them plates of chitin clashed and spread, their margins jagged to serve as teeth.

Cormac thrust upward into the mouth. The jawplates closed on his sword, gripping it firmly. Steel shrieked as the Gael drove the point further by main force.

The centipede tossed its head and flung Cormac thirty feet in the air. He bounced off the creature's curving back, then crashed down onto the heap of rubble. His helmet flew into the cavern. He still held his sword and, for a wonder, his buckler.

Cormac got to his feet as the centipede circled like a river of gleaming bone. Sticky juices streaked his blade, but he knew he hadn't stabbed deep enough to do serious damage. The centipede's body was so thick that he wasn't sure he *could* reach a vital spot.

The monster wasn't used to steel weapons, nor to a swordarm as strong as that of Cormac Mac Art. The creature would, nonetheless, crush and devour the man just as surely as the sun rose and set in the world beyond this hellpit wrenched out of time. . . .

The centipede started toward him. Cormac poised.

"Cormac!" bellowed a familiar voice.

Cormac's sword rang against the centipede's headshield, rupturing another of the bulging eyes. Powerful hands gripped beneath his armpits and lifted him bodily.

The centipede's head and forequarters rose effortlessly, fluidly. The mandibles spread like the jaws of a spring trap. Drops of pale venom winked on the hollow tips. The remaining antenna, longer than the Gael's body, nodded forward.

Cormac brought his Roman blade around in a sideways stroke that didn't endanger the man who held him from behind. His edge sang on the feathery chitin, severing the antenna near its midpoint and sending the fragment out into the trampled slime.

The centipede flowed forward unaffected. Cormac shouted and drew his knees up against his chest. The creature's mandibles clacked together like the lock of a catapult releasing.

Cormac slashed down between his feet. The blow swiped only air. He and the man holding him swayed abruptly upward, pulled by numbers of folk on the surface above the hole in the ceiling.

The centipede quivered over the mound of soil and bones, returning in the direction from which it had appeared. The beast had either given up once its prey rose above the height to which it could comfortably reach, or its damaged vision had lost Cormac in the relatively bright light streaming through the roof of the cavern.

Fresh body segments slid past all the time that Cormac dangled from the hole. The claws, scissoring forward in perfect rhythm, sounded like skeletons tumbling down a scree of other bones.

The Gael's head rose at last above the surface of the ring island. A large fish slapped nearby, in the belt of water. The foliage was rich and full, though the light of the false sun gave it a cast Cormac found unpleasant. After the guardian who prowled the tunnels below, however . . .

A pair of brown-skinned children stared at the Gael wide-eyed. The adults were all tugging on the rope which had raised Wulfhere and Cormac to safety.

Wulfhere released Cormac, who stepped thankfully to solid ground. The Gael's knees wobbled with reaction to the stress just ended. The pain in his rib cage was cold fire.

The Dane stood arms akimbo, grinning. "I figured you'd be coming," he said. "Matter of fact, I was going down to look for you. The folks here who saved me from that Greek wizard—"

Wulfhere gestured with his big thumb toward the dozen savages behind him. They were rubbing their palms where the rope had rubbed the skin into incipient blisters. One of them, a very young woman, wore an ornately-beaded vest and carried the wand of power thrust beneath the tie of her breechclout. She stepped up beside the Dane.

"—didn't think it was a good idea; but I thought it was a better idea than having you down there alone with our leggy friend."

Cormac took a deep breath. He shot his sword home in its sheath.

"You were both right," he said.

"I am Loughra," said the girl with the wand of power. "I am Queen of Atlantis, now that my brother is dead."

Thus far her voice was animated by a sense of cold pride. She looked around her domain—fleshy vegetation, two children, and a double handful of adults. In a sudden break which reminded Cormac of how young she really was, Loughra added, "We're all dead, now or shortly. Kanin and the others wouldn't let me take the wand when we fled. It was my right."

She glared at her fellows. Most of them were her seniors. Several were in their seventies or even older, though their features lacked the preternatural ancientness with which the wand branded those who used it.

"It was my right!" Loughra shouted.

The other Atlanteans stared at their hands or the far distance. They had the look of survivors of a beaten army ... as indeed they were. Between those slaughtered when they attacked the palace and the numbers the Guardian or wand had devoured in the cavern, most of the tribe had died this day.

Cormac eyed the savages. Now that he was among rescuers rather than trading blows in blood-spattered chaos, he was struck by their high foreheads and the craftsmanship displayed in their dress and equipment.

One of the band held a steel-headed spear whose seven-foot shaft was reinforced with metal strips for half its length. The broad blade was inlaid with runes of silver.

Ichor from the centipede dulled the runes carved into the steel. The Atlantean wiped at it with a wad of bark cloth.

Wulfhere followed Cormac's eyes. "Yes, Aslief's," the Dane agreed. "We'll meet in Valhalla, it seems, but not before. Gorm was honored to fall to such a foe."

Cormac looked at his friend in surprise.

"Aslief the Saxon came to us just before Hotin and Balla were born," Loughra explained, nodding toward the pair of children. Two-year-olds, Cormac guessed. It would be difficult to tell time in a place without day, night or seasons.

"He and his men fought their way past the wizards who would have drained them as they do all their captives. The Saxons built a raft, but the water monsters tipped it and took all but Aslief himself. We healed his wounds, and at the end he led us against the wizards."

"The oily bastard Creon who choked me silly with his blue light?" Wulfhere said. "He's not the descendant of the wizards who came here all that time ago. He and his daughter *are* those wizards. They drink the blood of everyone they catch to keep themselves young."

The Dane's finger unconsciously traced the hammer rune on the flat of his axe.

"Not the blood but the life," Loughra corrected. "Though it comes to the same thing. Aslief led us through the tunnels. He fought the Guardian while the rest of us opened the way into the palace."

"A good job, that," Wulfhere said softly as his finger moved. "I hadn't really seen the leggy one—"

To avoid omen, the Dane didn't say "the Guardian," though that was merely a title rather than a name.

"—until I went down after you. Handling him for however long with a spear was man's work.

"Poseidon has forsaken us," Loughra said miserably. "He caused the monsters—"

Creon and Antheia, not the beasts in the water and cavern; and from what Cormac now believed, the term was well applied.

"—to be prepared with their magic when we arrived. Otherwise we would have ended their reign forever!"

It wasn't just the Greeks' magic that turned the attack into a catastrophe, Cormac realized uneasily. A moment before he had thought the eyes of the Atlantean survivors were dull, torpid. Now his mind put a sinister cast on their expressions.

"I have no friends on the other side of a battle line!" Cormac said harshly. He eased his right foot backward, to brace him if he needed to clear his sword in the next instant. "Whatever he may have been before or become since."

Wulfhere stepped close to the Gael and hugged him, pinning his arms. "The folk here kept me tied while they carried me through the tunnels," the Dane rumbled. "Otherwise I would have killed them all before they could explain they were rescuing me . . . and the one with legs would have eaten me as he did Aslief, like as not."

Wulfhere released his friend.

"It was Poseidon's will," said Loughra. "You were no more than his instrument."

"A big fellow, Aslief," Wulfhere said with a grimly reflective expression on his face. His eyes were focused well beyond the artificial horizon. "His flesh delayed the leggy one for some time, even after it had gotten past his spear."

Cormac stretched his powerful arms up and back, working the weight of his armor loose from the grooves it dug in his muscles as he stood motionless. Something large shrieked half a mile away. He remembered the elephant skull in the cavern beneath.

"The folk here say there's no way out," Wulfhere said without emotional loading. "That much of the Greeks' story was true. They say we can stay here with them on the island."

"There are no children born here any more," Loughra said. "Hotin and Balla were the last, and before them none for—half my lifetime. Poseidon has forsaken us."

The elephant trumpeted again. Cormac looked at the Atlantean queen, but his mind considered all the threads of the net that knotted about him.

The ring of water was broad and deep enough to be a world in itself. The creatures there would live and breed for so long as the bubble that was Atlantis remained. There was no realistic chance that men could live to cross it. That Aslief had done so was a comment on the number of Saxons whom he'd led: more meat than there were hungry maws to devour it.

The cavern was another matter. Hard-shelled creatures could live indefinitely without food. Cormac had once found a spider beneath a helmet which had been rusting for at least three years. The helmet rim, stamped into the wet soil during a massacre, blocked any potential prey—but the spider, silent and patient, waited nonetheless alive in its ragged web.

Creon and Antheia spoke of "the Guardian" as if the centipede were as old as they were; but also as if it were alone. A single creature could be killed; but not, Cormac judged from his own experience, by weapons in the hands of two pirates and the surviving Atlanteans.

Something had to be done. The Greeks, like bad husbandmen, had cropped the fittest of their herd of servants for millennia so that now only stunted rejects remained. Forced by circumstances of their own creation, Creon and his daughter had turned their powers beyond the boundaries of the world in which they were trapped, snatching folk out of the sea.

Irishmen, Saxons; the leaders of a band of Danish pirates.

"Speaking for myself . . ." Wulfhere said, watching the Gael sidelong; waiting for cues on a visage which for the moment was as quiet as cast bronze. ". . . I just want to get out of this place."

"That was all I wanted before," Cormac whispered. "Now—I still want to leave. But first we'll put an end to the folk who brought us here, not so, my friend?"

He looked at Wulfhere and smiled. It was a terrible expression.

The Dane shrugged his mighty shoulders and smiled back. "If you want it so much, why not?" he said. "I've killed people for less."

Wulfhere laughed, the audible equivalent of the Gael's visage. "I've killed people to test the edge of a new sword!"

The reivers clasped their right arms; hand to elbow, wrist to wrist. They both laughed. In a moment the distant elephant trumpeted again in frightened surmise.

"This is madness!" Loughra cried in sudden fury as she watched the reivers' preparations. "You'll die for no reason!"

Her words echoed unconsciously those of Creon when he realized Cormac was determined to follow the Dane's captors into the tunnels. The humor of the thought was no more than the quiver of butterfly wings around the grim monolith of Cormac's concentration, but it was present to that extent.

Wulfhere checked the balance of the spear which had been Aslief's. Spears weren't the Dane's weapon of choice, but neither was the centipede a normal opponent.

"A man can die but once," he said without concern. "And besides, Othinn loves brave men."

"We won't help you with this!" Loughra said. "If you stayed here with us—perhaps the monsters' spell against children won't work on you and, and . . ."

"No one asked you for help," Cormac said. He ignored the remainder of the girl's—the woman's—statement. The first female he'd gotten involved with on Atlantis had nearly brought his death. He wasn't sure that Loughra was a safer bet than Antheia had been; and anyway, he had other business.

The Gael braced his heels against the ground and tugged with all his strength at the cords of bull sinew which anchored the rope ladder to three separate trees. Aslief had constructed the ladder to accept his weight and that of the entire Atlantean raiding party climbing down behind him, but Cormac believed in being doubly sure when that was possible.

"It would make a fine saga, would it not?" Wulfhere commented. "How the two of us went into the dragon's cave and fought him?"

Wulfhere eyed his axe critically. He buffed the steel on his trouser leg. He'd worked on the edge with an oilstone for an hour, though he hadn't used the weapon since a raid in the Orkneys nearly a month earlier. Creon's snare of blue light had caught the Dane with no target for his steel and fury.

"Of course," he added, "it isn't really a dragon. And

there won't be anyone left to write the saga. But it would be a fine one."

"We aren't going to fight anything if we're lucky," Cormac muttered. "Down and back, that's all."

He looked at the ladder and their equipment, then to his hulking friend. "The gear's ready," Cormac said. "Are you?"

"To *not* fight?" Wulfhere said. "But whatever you say, little man. You understand more of this business than I do."

Cormac kicked the ladder into the opening. Bamboo battens stiffened the rungs, though cross-ropes would provide support even if a rung cracked under the reivers' weight. The hollow wood clattered now.

Cormac dropped hand-over-hand into the glowing cavern.

Cormac's boots hit the pile of rubble. The vast cavity was filled as before by an echoing sigh. It would fade to the impression of silence in a few moments, deadening the way the sound of surf on a rocky strand did. That was dangerous, because the background the mind taught itself to discount was still loud enough to conceal the approach of an enemy.

Conceal the approach of the Guardian.

Cormac pivoted his head as he jumped clear. Wulfhere crashed to the ground with an angry grunt. The Dane's axe was jagged lightning in a battle, but climbing wasn't a skill on which the big man prided himself.

"What now?" he demanded, checking around him as the Gael had done. "You're not planning to fight, but the one with the legs may have his own ideas."

"This way," Cormac said, loping off the ramp and along the quay. "We're going to pull down one of the pillars farther down the tunnel."

"With ourselves beneath it?" Wulfhere muttered. There was a touch of perverse pride in his voice. "Well, I said I'd follow."

There was no sign of the centipede. The creature had a huge area to patrol. They could do their work and be out before it found them.

"What's wrong with this one?" Wulfhere asked peevishly as Cormac led him past a pillar. The Dane didn't like to run any more than he liked climbing.

"Not far enough," Cormac said, though it was a pity. The top half of the pillar was skewed at a 30° angle, and a vertical crack ran from there to the ground. It would be easy to complete the job earth tremors had started; but that wouldn't do any good.

"Why didn't you tell the folk above what you planned?" Wulfhere said. "Why make a secret of it?"

"They wouldn't have helped," the Gael said. The truth was that his paranoid need for secrecy was deeper than his rationalizations of it, though there was truth in the rationalizations too. "They might have tried to hinder. Our reasons aren't theirs."

The next pillar was fifty yards farther on. Cormac hoped it would do. Each echoing clack of his hobnails flashed an image of the centipede into his mind.

"This one!" he said. He thrust his prybar between two tilted courses of the pillar's masonry.

The savages made their tools and weapons from the cladding of ruined buildings—bronze, tin, copper, and brass so pale it might almost pass for gold. They had no iron or steel, but this bar was of sturdy bronze stiffened by cruciform ridges.

Perhaps the centipede wouldn't be able to sense the reivers because its antennae were injured.

Perhaps a Druid would appear, make a pass with his golden sickle, and snatch Cormac and the Dane back into the world where they belonged.

Wulfhere eyed the situation, then thrust the point of Aslief's spear beside the prybar. He twisted and, without seeming effort, levered onto the floor an ashlar that outweighed him.

The block hit with a crash, skipped on one corner,

and finally lay flat. Cormac inserted his bar vertically between stones of the next course up. He pried, easing his weight onto the tool until the full tigerish strength of his muscles was deployed. The bronze bent, though he'd inserted the bar deep enough that the fulcrum was on the fat part.

Wulfhere thrust, leaned into his spear, and grunted. The block sprang free. The stone beside it sagged loose and followed. A quick jerk from Cormac's tool wrenched a block from the lower course.

The masonry was set without mortar. The pillars' core was concrete and aggregate, shattered ages past by the torquing as Atlantis sank. All the reivers had to do was to strip a course from the ashlar sheathing and the ceiling's weight would—

The centipede, a darkness spattering glowing dollops of fungus from its claws, swept down on them.

"Finish the job!" Cormac shouted. He dropped the prybar, drew his sword, and reached behind his left hip for the slung buckler. The command and the complex of movements came from his subconscious. "I'll hold him!"

"No!" boomed Wulfhere, dragging the spear free of the crevice into which he'd inserted it for the next stage of the demolition work.

"Our only chance is to bring the roof down, you boneheaded Dane!" Cormac screamed. Waving his shield high above him, he took three accelerating steps to meet the centipede.

The creature paused, lifting its head and three foremost body segments against the shield's perceived threat. Cormac ducked low. Mandibles clashed above his head.

He was in a forest of legs, hair-tufted and jagged with chitinous edges. The Gael cut to the right and backhanded left. His bright steel bit through the flexible membrane covering a joint.

Ichor, transparent and of no color but that of the

fungus glow, dripped from the rent. The lower leg dangled limp.

The centipede curled back on itself like a wave rebounding. The mandibles were cocked for another stroke. Jaw-plates clashed and reopened behind the poison-dripping points. As soon as the creature attacked, its limited brain function put in motion all the apparatus of eating.

Cormac dived, shouldering aside the injured limb. He rolled to his feet again just clear of the centipede's flowing form. Its head slid beneath body segments in a chitinous knot. The centipede's damaged eyes and antennae—the olfactory receptors—prevented it from spotting its prey again for a moment.

Masonry crashed in a miniature avalanche, a dozen blocks or more in rapid succession. Wulfhere worked with spear and prybar simultaneously. The Dane was attacking the pillar with the same precision and casual strength that he would have displayed while demolishing a hostile shield wall.

If he was aware of Cormac and the centipede, he gave no sign of the fact.

Cormac breathed in shuddering gulps. The centipede located him and came on again. The stumps of its antennae waved.

The Gael stepped toward the creature. His stride wasn't as firm as he'd expected. His right boot slid on the fungus coating.

The centipede's head whipped around in a quick arc, slamming its mandibles into Cormac from the left side. The shield held, but the arm holding it went numb. The blow flung him down, skidding and spinning across the stones.

The centipede came on. Its claws clicked like blades of the mechanical harvesters of Northern Gaul. Cormac kicked, trying to swing so that his armored torso protected his bare legs from the yard-long mandibles.

Wulfhere grabbed the Gael by the shoulder and dragged him clear with neither hesitation nor delicacy. The centipede's tons of rippling mass hit the pillar with the violence of a ship being launched.

The wobbling masonry collapsed, showering down in chunks that would crush any man, armored or no. The centipede's legs continued to row the creature forward, unaffected by the blocks and massive fragments which glanced from its chitinous back.

Cormac scrambled away on all fours—his boots, his shield, and the knuckles of his sword hand. The buckler rang like a gong each time it hit the floor, but not even Cormac could hear it over the continuing destruction of ancient Atlantis.

The metal ceiling sagged after the crumbling pillar, then tore. Water sprayed down, increasing to a torrent. The reivers had succeeded: the caverns here lay beneath the moat, not solid ground.

It remained to be seen whether the two of them would escape to savor their victory.

The Dane was kneeling nearby, gripping to his belly a block with one concave side. It had been part of the pillar's flaring capital.

For an instant, Cormac couldn't imagine what his friend was doing. Then he realized that the massive stone had taken a hop toward Wulfhere and that the Dane had trapped it between his torso and the ground instead of letting it smash over and past him. The shock knocked the breath from his body.

Cormac lifted his friend, though he didn't dare sheathe his sword or drop the buckler. He thrust his blade and right hand beneath the Dane's arm and dragged him up, off the block that had nearly killed him.

"Come on, you lazy scut!" Cormac shouted. "How am I supposed to get out of here without you to carry me?"

Mud, reeds, and something that flapped in and out

of the fallen water like a tossed coin cascaded with the torrent through the ceiling. The spread of the influx was easily measured by the degree to which darkness displaced the fungus glow. Faint phosphorescence glimmered through the first touch of water, but any quantity of the muddy fluid choked and poisoned the light.

Wulfhere staggered forward, though he was bent over and breathed in short gasps. He'd lost Aslief's spear. His left hand lay on Cormac's hip so that the Gael could guide their paired flight. Wulfhere's mind and body had both been stunned by the blow. He could follow a friend's lead, and at need he could fight.

The axe was in the Dane's right hand. Wulfhere Skull-splitter could always fight.

Water raced ankle-deep over the cavern's floor. The surface was even more treacherous than the slime of fungus had made it before. Sharp tearing sounds punctuated the roar of water. The torrent was expanding the hole through which it drained, gouging out the ring's underpinning fabric once its integrity had been breached.

A blaze of purple-green light marked their goal. The illumination was almost painfully bright to eyes adapted for the soft omnipresence of the fungus. The rope ladder swayed gently in a breeze driven by the rush of water displacing air from the cavern.

Wulfhere took his hand from Cormac's side and turned with his axe lifting. Cormac felt his friend's motion and rotated with him reflexively, as the two of them had done on a hundred battlefields before.

The centipede rushed toward them in a spray thrown by its pulsing legs.

Cormac shouted and waved his shield in the creature's face. The centipede reared as it had done before. The bundles of ganglia that served it as a brain were able to react in only one fashion to a stimulus, no matter how frequently that stimulus was repeated. Wulfhere, swinging with both hands and stepping into the stroke, sheared off the right-hand leg of the fourth body segment.

The centipede came down on the Gael, ignoring the swordslash aimed between head and body. Cormac's blade nicked the chitin of the headshield, but the joint was too well protected to be damaged by a sword.

Legs pinned Cormac on his back in slopping water. The mandibles scissored together. His buckler's plywood core shattered under the repeated contact. The right mandible pierced it, tearing along Cormac's wrist. The Gael shouted and stabbed upward, blinded by his buckler jerking in front of his eyes on the poison fang.

Wulfhere chopped, drew clear, and chopped again. Each blow left a leg dangling by a few shreds of chitinous armor. The Dane was withdrawing his axe for a fourth stroke, as methodical as a woodcutter, when the centipede whipped to escape an attack that even its mass was forced to recognize.

The Dane helped Cormac up with his left hand. He held the axe raised in his right and never took his eyes off the centipede. The creature circled the two men and the pile of rubble. Its long body had a brownish cast in the light falling through the hole in the cavern roof.

"You all right?" Wulfhere asked. Back to back, the companions began to climb the ramp. The centipede rippled past, its legs pulsing hypnotically. At any moment it would come on again.

"I'll do," Cormac said. He flexed his left hand. The mandible had bruised him when it smashed through his shield, but the skin was unbroken. He was limping slightly. Foreleg pincers had torn the muscles of both thighs.

The pair reached the top of the rubble pile. As

soon as one of the men started to climb the ladder, the centipede would be over the other like surf on sand.

"You get up that ladder," Cormac ordered harshly. "I'll be right behind you."

"Your mother's a whore," said the Dane. "You were first down, you'll be first up. Get moving!"

The water was knee deep across all visible parts of the cavern. Its rushing flow ate at the edges of the ramp. A further section of roof followed the fallen pillar into the cataract.

The centipede drove up the ramp on scores of uninjured legs, its mandibles wide. The reivers shifted apart, giving each room to use his weapon unimpeded. Wulfhere lifted his axe two-handed over his right shoulder.

Cormac braced his right foot behind him, prepared this time to thrust with the full weight of his body behind the swordpoint. He didn't know whether his steel would turn or break or drive straight through the headshield, and he was sure that even with what passed for a brain removed the centipede would live long enough to kill and eat the both of them. A man must fight, even when he knows he cannot win.

A small figure dropped from the rope ladder and darted between the men: Loughra, the wand in her right hand. Its blue glare lighted her body as it wrapped the oncoming centipede in threads that not even the monster's armored strength could break. The girl aged as swiftly as salt melts in a puddle.

Cormac started toward her. Wulfhere grabbed the Gael's arm with his left hand.

Cormac turned. "Let me go!" he shouted.

Wulfhere dragged him back toward the ladder. "Come on!" he said. "It's too late for her."

Cormac tried to club the Dane with the pommel of his sword. Wulfhere blocked the blow with his axe helve. "Come on!" he repeated.

Wulfhere was right. Loughra, a 17-year-old girl when she jumped from the ladder, now crouched as a toothless crone in the blaze of her wand. The centipede's legs thrashed furiously, unable to break the grip of the blue web clinging to its head and forward body segments. The power required to freeze the tons of rapacious carnivore was enormous—

As was the cost of that power. A surge of water driven by a further collapse of the ceiling tugged at Loughra's waist and almost dragged her down with it.

Cormac sheathed his sword and leaped for the ladder. The rungs were set a foot and a half apart. Cormac took them two at a time, hurling himself up onto the surface like wax blown from a jar of beer stoppered too early. The battens flexed but did not break under his step.

An ongoing geyser of muddy water spewed from the belt of water, high enough that Cormac could see it above the vegetation surrounding the sinkhole. He drew his sword. None of Loughra's tribe was present.

Wulfhere clambered up to the surface beside him, panting like a blown horse. The Dane's legs were wet to the knees.

The ground shook. An enormous jet of water shot twice as high as the previous norm, then sank back out of sight. The bottom must have dropped from acres of the ring lake. Water surged nearly to the sinkhole's lip.

"Now's the time to cross on the dry bottom," the Gael said. He bent and braced his hands on his knees to make it easier to draw in the breaths for which his lungs burned. "Before they're expecting us. Creon and Antheia."

A four-horned deer sprinted through the undergrowth, thrown into blind panic by destruction on a geological scale. Cormac didn't know what draining the lake into the cavern would do to Atlantis in the long term, nor did he care. In the short term, it would permit Cormac to get within the length of his sword of the Greek who brought him here.

The centipede, swirling in the currents raging below, gripped the lip of the sinkhole with a foreleg. It had managed to shed Cormac's shield from its mandible. Its jawplates worked furiously on the remnants of Atlantis' last queen.

Cormac's sword slashed the joint articulating the pincered foot. Wulfhere reversed his axe and drove the back of it as a hammer into the creature's headshield. The chitin around the right-hand cluster of eyes, damaged by the Gael's sword in the cavern below, shattered like a terra-cotta pot.

Another leg reached up to replace the first. The Dane had in the cavern severed the forelimbs on the other side.

Cormac sliced this leg off at the last joint also. Wulfhere brought his blade around in a figure-eight, putting the edge deep into the pulpy mass where he had crushed the armor.

The centipede slid away from the opening, rolling onto its back as it disappeared. The jaws still masticated their prey, but Loughra had defeated the monster before she died.

"Yes," said Wulfhere through his gasping inhalations. "Let's go kill Greeks. Would there were more than two."

The bed of the ring lake was knee-deep in soupy mud. Eventually the sediment might dry out or slurp after the water into the caverns, but Cormac hadn't had the time to waste. Cursing and holding his sword high to keep it clean, he tramped toward the central citadel with Wulfhere beside him.

A fish five yards long flopped wildly nearby. Its jaws could easily swallow a man. A bad hop might bring the fish down on top of the reivers, but its mind was

no longer on food. The false sun threw a sickly hue
across the creature's silvery scales.

The carrion feeders would feast tonight.

They were hallway across the ring. The march was
exhausting and had already taken far longer than Cormac had allowed for. Creon and Antheia would have
time to prepare for the reivers' return, though the
Gael could hope that other aspects of the disaster
would absorb the Greeks' attention.

It didn't matter. The way Cormac felt now, he
would have charged a shield wall, naked and bare-
handed.

"That wand is well lost where it can't kill more folk
the way it's done so many," he snarled suddenly. "She
didn't have to do that!"

"Nor did we," the Dane said. "Who knows why a
man does a thing? Even a *man*."

Wulfhere's boots squelched up and down in a
steady beat. Cormac rushed forward in bursts of
twenty yards or so, then waited panting to recruit his
strength before sprinting another stretch.

The marble coping which surrounded the central
island had stood a foot and a half above the previous
water level. Now the men could see that in addition
there was twice that height of stone discolored by
algae, and the glistening depth of muck besides. The
whole combined in a sheer height greater than Cormac wanted to clamber after struggling in armor
through the gooey bottom.

A hundred yards to the right of the reivers'
intended approach stood a half-ruined marble gazebo,
above a staircase down into what had been the water.
The Gael changed his angle to intersect the structure.
Beyond it loomed the back of a silver-clad building
which he supposed was the palace.

A shelled and tentacled creature lay half-submerged
in the mud nearby. More than a score of ten-foot
arms lay flaccid on the surface. Cormac thought for

a moment that the creature was dead, but he noticed that the pupil of its lidless eye was tracking him. He made sure that their path was beyond the arms' radius.

Wulfhere nodded toward the creature. "I suppose I'd rather tramp through mud," the Dane said, "than swim with things like that."

A scaly head appeared over the curve of the land. One eye caught the wading men. The head swivelled on a neck holding it ten feet in the air; both eyes focused on the potential prey.

The kronosaur hooted angrily and came slithering across the mud toward them.

"Or swim with that one," muttered Wulfhere. "Though walking with it may not be much better."

"Run!" Cormac shouted.

The men were a hundred yards from dry land where the advantage would be theirs. The kronosaur was at least five times as far from them, but the fifty-foot monster's paddle feet propelled it with reasonable efficiency through the mud. The beast couldn't survive the draining of the lake indefinitely, but it was alive now and furious as well as hungry.

Maybe if he and Wulfhere stood still where they were?

But the kronosaur had already marked its prey. Besides, their dragging footprints trailed through the mud behind them like a frozen wake.

The men shambled across the muck in slow motion. There was nothing heroic about being drowned in a slough or disappearing down a gullet sized for vastly larger fish.

"If we—" Wulfhere called.

"—reach the steps—" he went on. Words spurted out in clumps each time the Dane's right boot slopped down.

"—can you hold—"

"—the thing alone?"

"Yes!" Cormac snarled.

His world was fire, not mud. The muscles of his legs burned, his pumping arms burned, and the flames from his blazing chest curled up and threw a blood-red filter across his eyes.

The Gael didn't know what Wulfhere intended, nor did he care. He was completely focused on reaching the protection of the gazebo before the kronosaur gulped him down. He was also completely certain that he wouldn't succeed, that he would die in a lizard's gut and worse, that he would *fail—*

Cormac's hobnails clashed on the marble stairs. Up two, up two more. Well out of the mud, firm footing for a battle.

Cormac spun. The Dane clumped past him, splashing mud on the steps as his boots slammed down. The kronosaur, heaving a ten-foot bow wave through the greasy muck, darted its head toward the men. The tongue shot out. It was forked and black-veined against spongy magenta flesh.

Cormac's sword described a perfect arc that flicked off one lobe of the tongue. Blood sprayed.

The kronosaur jerked back its head and clopped its long jaws shut over the damaged organ. Its chest throbbed, expelling waste air in twin funnels of vapor from the nostrils above its eyesockets. The flaps that closed the air passages during dives pulsed open and shut within each breath cycle.

Cormac backed two steps upward, then two more. The monster came on again. Its back was covered in black scales with a green undercoat. Rosette patterns glowed in the light of the false sun.

The tip of Cormac's blade ripped across the gums of the kronosaur's upper jaw. It wasn't a dangerous wound, but nothing the Gael could achieve with a sword *could* endanger a something the size of this creature.

Pain snatched the huge head back with a high-pitched bellow. Unlike the centipede, the reptile had enough brain cells to react to being hurt. Sword-pricks, however expertly placed, wouldn't stop the kronosaur forever, but they encouraged the beast to caution.

Cormac backed, placing each foot precisely. If he slipped, it would be over in an eyeblink. He reached the top of the staircase. The gazebo's domed roof had collapsed, but most of the columns still stood. They offered protection against the creature's darting thrusts.

The kronosaur hunched, then advanced like a land slip. It propelled itself by matched rearward strokes of its front paddles. The smaller hind paddles provided little besides rudder effect. The great body crashed into the staircase, shattering and displacing the ancient marble. The head lanced down like that of a starling taking a grub.

Cormac jumped forward beneath the attack and thrust up into the kronosaur's throat. The beast's powerful neck muscles were iron-hard. The Gael's point bit but turned a hand's breadth deep, gouging a broad bloody track instead of cutting a vein or the windpipe.

The creature shrieked in fury and tossed its head. The jaws had found a pillar when they missed their intended prey. The kronosaur's teeth were squat cones with rounded tips, very thick at the base. They were optimized for crushing the shells of armored cuttlefish like the creature the reivers had skirted near the shore.

The teeth ground marble with the same relentless power that was intended for calcite shells. Stone flaked and crumbled. The shaft was constructed of separate cylinders connected internally by lead cramps. The kronosaur shook its head, flinging the stone barrels wildly as the metal tore.

The beast humped its body for a further advance. The kronosaur was clumsy on dry land, but it was by no means inert. The paddles swept forward, throwing the Gael twenty feet up the slope when one chanced to swipe him as he tried to thrust again.

The kronosaur's eyes and instincts tracked Cormac as a motion. The head swung in, jaws open. The teeth would make as little account of chain mail as they did of powdering a stone pillar.

An arrow pinned the forked tongue to the lower palate.

The kronosaur screamed and raised its head to locate the new enemy. Wulfhere stood on a walkway of overgrown marble slabs, halfway down from the palace. His bow was in his hands. As Cormac scrambled to his feet, the Dane loosed another arrow into the reptile's open mouth.

The kronosaur bellowed and heaved itself through the ruined gazebo, smashing the eight-inch columns still standing in its haste to reach its tormentor. It hurt the beast to shift its weight on dry ground with paddles, but the creature moved with clumsy speed nonetheless.

Cormac stabbed behind the ribs as the creature wallowed past. Because he thrust against the grain of the scales, his blade sank nearly the length of his forearm into the reptile's flesh. The wound had no evident effect.

Wulfhere held his ground as coolly as he would in the face of a charge by armored cavalry. The long Danish bow snapped an arrow deep in the ridge of bone above the kronosaur's right eyesocket, then another into the eye itself.

The beast twisted its head and slewed right. Its primeval brain was unable to compensate swiftly for the loss of binocular vision.

Wulfhere, regular as the drips of a waterclock, shot into the creature's throat. Arrows sank to their fletching when they struck the creases which permitted the neck to flex.

Cormac set his right boot against the kronosaur's side for the leverage he needed to withdraw his sword. He succeeded, but it was like pulling the blade from living rock.

The beast turned toward him with the massive abruptness of a landslide. The Gael made an instant decision. He hurled himself toward and under the huge body. Belly plates scraped his boot as he rolled clear. The kronosaur's bulk slammed down on the spot Cormac had been standing a moment before.

It hadn't been attacking him: it was trying to get away. Wulfhere's arrows had the effect of hornet stings on a human; and, like hornets, they were as potentially lethal in sufficient number.

The Dane paused. He had an arrow nocked, but he wasn't tensing the bowstring of human hair. The kronosaur hurled itself back onto the lakebed with a vast outspewing of cushioning mud.

"Good work with that—" Cormac began.

Wulfhere lifted and drew the bow with a smooth motion, his arms working together. He loosed the shaft at the moment of maximum tension. The arrow's flight was almost too swift for human eyes to mark. A tuft of goose-quill fletching sprang from the back of the kronosaur's head, where the foramen magnum opened to pass the spinal cord into the skull.

The beast continued to flop forward across the lake bottom. Its muscles were controlled only by the autonomic nervous system, the way a headless chicken runs.

Wulfhere cast down his bow. That had been his last arrow.

Cormac massaged his right wrist with his left hand. Stabbing so deeply through tough muscle had put enormous strain on those muscles and small bones. "It was already running away," he said.

"Yes," the Dane said. "Now we know that it won't come back."

Cormac shrugged, then stripped a handful of leaves with which to clean reptile blood from his blade. "Let's go find some Greeks," he said.

Earthshocks made foliage tremble as the reivers approached the rear of the palace. A thick silver plate shook from its mounting rivets and clanged to the walkway ahead of them.

Wulfhere chuckled. "They think we're come to collect a debt owed," he said.

"And so we are," Cormac said. His voice was as thin as the light dancing along the edge of his sword.

The door was a recent replacement panel of wood and leather. It hung open as the Dane had left it when he rushed through to retrieve his bow and quiver. He hadn't had time to worry then about what was waiting within. The reivers entered now with tense caution, weapons ready and bodies tautly prepared to spring into lethal action.

No one was in the service suite just inside the door. The next chamber was the dining room. The bodies of savages killed during the raid had vanished, but blood and the wrecked furniture remained. Heavy rubbish—broken marble statues and the base of a large column—had been piled over the hole in the flooring.

A pair of stunted servants stood looking out through the far door, whispering to one another. They squealed and tried to run when the reivers appeared behind them. Cormac made a tigerish leap and caught the female before she could escape.

Wulfhere bent toward the captive. "Where are your masters?" he shouted. The Atlantean covered her face with both hands and keened in a high-pitched voice.

"I'll handle it," Cormac said. Though they didn't have a language in common . . .

He lifted the servant to her feet. She weighed no more than a normal child. For that matter, she might *be* a child. All her folk had wizened features, reminding Cormac of the toll exacted by the wizardry used here.

"Creon?" he said, trying not to snarl in a threatening fashion. "Antheia? Listen to me, child."

He tried to keep tone soothing though the words themselves could not be. She ought to recognize the names, at least.

"Where are Creon and Antheia?"

The captive continued to cry. The male servant unexpectedly poked his head around the doorjamb and chittered. He pumped his small arm, pointing behind him with his index and middle fingers extended together.

Cormac released the female servant. The reivers glided together through the door. Their Atlantean guide scampered ahead, giving the bigger men looks of obvious terror over his shoulder. He ran out the front door of the palace and pointed again, this time toward the temple beyond.

"Right, let's go," the Dane muttered. He broke into a heavy-footed jog, the best speed of which he was capable. Cormac matched him in an easy lope. The Gael bent his right arm so that the swordblade swayed gently in front of his body.

The servant guide cowered beside the entrance as the reivers passed. When Cormac looked back to check possible pursuit, he saw the Atlantean couple hugging one another in the doorway.

The earth chuckled to itself. Blocks of the courtyard's paving chipped their edges together and hopped a hand's breadth in the air.

Cormac extended his stride to enter the temple just ahead of his companion. There was no one present in the nave, though legions could have concealed themselves in the pillared aisles.

The dome was a thunderous echo chamber, but the source of the vast booming was in the vaults underneath.

The door from which the Greeks had initially
appeared was at the far end of the building. It hung
open again.

"This way," called Cormac. He realized that he
couldn't hear his own voice, though that didn't matter:
Wulfhere had seen the doorway on his own.

The men paused to right and left of the portal,
bringing their breathing under control before they
went to the next stage. A spiral staircase led down.
The metal was lustrously silver in color but untarnished through the ages since it was built. The backless treads and slender balustrades vibrated like
hummingbirds' wings in the noise surrounding them.
The reivers couldn't see the floor from the angle at
which they stood.

Cormac slipped through the doorway an instant
before Wulfhere committed himself. The helical staircase was only wide enough for one man at a time.

The treads augered down for hundreds of feet to
a surface of water lifted into standing waves by thunderous vibration. Purple-green lights like miniatures
of the false sun depended from nodes on the walls.
They were shaking also.

Huge silvery spheres spun in the hollow volume
without any material support. The water had risen to
bathe their lower sides, making the rotation noticeably
erratic. Froth whipped by the globes' touch flew as
high as the doorway.

Cormac would have missed Creon and Antheia in
the chaotic hugeness were it not for the spiteful blue
light that drew his eyes. The Greeks' tiny figures and
their undamaged power device were near one side of
the circular chamber.

The walls had begun to buckle under the thrust of
water filling the dockyard caverns beyond. Water
shifted blocks inward and spewed between the inter-
stices. Antheia was attempting to push the heavy
stones back into place with threads of blue fire.

The scale of the catastrophe was beyond the capacity of the Greeks' remaining tool. For so long as someone's life force energized it, the device could withstand the pressure; but the water was patient and omnipresent. If one path was blocked, it would find another . . .

A form that must be Creon's bobbed on the surface beside the device. The tool had stripped him to a husk that floated like pith.

Antheia, as shrunken as a fly drained in a spider's web, stood at the controls. She turned her face toward the doorway above. She tried to lift an arm, but she lacked the strength.

Cormac thought of Loughra in the jaws of the centipede. He did not smile, but there was no pity in his heart.

The blue glare vanished. A hundred feet of wall burst inward before a rush of water. Balls spun into one another, disintegrating in vivid violet light.

Wulfhere tugged the Gael's arm insistently. The reivers retreated into the nave.

Cormac slammed the door closed, but the rumbling sound was the whole world. A pillar fell from somewhere in the clerestory. It shattered on the floor like a bomb. The reivers ran by mutual instinct toward an aisle. That was the shortest distance out of the huge structure, though there was no certain safety outside either.

The floor beneath the dome buckled upward in a rolling motion, like that of a hound shaking its loose skin. Massive hexagonal paving blocks flipped and fell. The pillars began to sway.

Cormac sprinted across the thirty-foot aisle. The parallel lines of columns nodded their tops together, then away. The nave imploded as trusses cracked. Chunks of the coffered dome cascaded down like snowflakes in a blizzard.

The flat roof above the aisle ripped along its axis.

The outer line of columns shook a few of its ornate capitals onto the courtyard beyond, then rocked inward again and collapsed toward the ruin of the nave. Stone barrels weighing a half ton each bounced and danced in the rubble, dwarfed by the scale of destruction around them.

Cormac, his long Roman blade quivering in his right hand, leaped off the temple slab in a flat dive. It was ten feet down from the slab to the courtyard when he leaped, six feet as the ground heaved up to meet him when he was halfway through the maneuver, ten feet again when he tucked and rolled. The slabs shook themselves and lifted the Gael to his feet as though he and the dying world were a pair of practiced acrobats.

The dome and its support columns had plunged into the vaults beneath the temple. Now a gout of high-pressure steam lifted thousands of tons of shattered stone back from the pit. Tunnel ceilings ruptured in a web of fog and destruction, displacing foliage and buildings already ruined by time.

"Wulfhere!" Cormac shouted vainly. The sound was a cataclysmic pressure that drove the very breath from his lungs. The Gael stumbled forward. Slabs slid one by one into the expanding crater which had already engulfed the temple.

The false sun grew dim—shaded by the gush of steam, Cormac thought; but more than that as well. The light's hue had changed from purple-green to saffron as pale as the flames above ill-vented coal.

"Wulfhere!"

The Dane's huge hand groped his. They clutched each other, left to left, because each had his weapon out in his right fist. There was nothing to fight here, but a man clings to what matters to him in the hour he knows to be his last.

An axe, a sword, and a friend as the world ends.

The false sun faded until it gave no more light than

the moon does in daytime. A distant roar penetrated from all directions, riding over the crackling destruction of the last of Atlantis.

The surface ruptured again at the edge of the courtyard. A pine hundreds of feet high toppled over and smashed to the ground a few yards from where the men stood. They didn't run. The tree was only a hint of motion in the non-light and besides, there was no place to run.

The sky shattered like a giant eggshell. The light of a normal sun, filtered by the mists of the northern seas of Earth, dissolved the tumbling shards. A foam-toothed wave surged from all margins of what remained of Atlantis, swallowing the land down inexorably.

Atlantis was sinking forever.

Cormac sheathed his sword with a clang of guard against the iron lip of its scabbard. They had a moment before the ground crumbled beneath them.

"Come on!" he cried to Wulfhere, tugging the Dane with him toward the tree which had nearly crushed them a moment ago. There was light now to move by.

The reivers threw themselves into the branches of the pine. Cormac thought of binding himself in with his sword belt, but he couldn't tell the attitude at which the tree would float. Besides, there wasn't enough time.

There was no time at all. A salt wave surged over them, pounding and washing the reivers clean of the taint of a world that should have died millennia before.

The tree surged, twisted, and started to roll. Cormac bellowed as the trunk rotated down. Salt water drowned what he expected to be his final shout of defiance. The massive trunk didn't crush him against the marble pavement after all. The ground had already vanished into the depths of the present sea.

The tree shuddered in decreasing arcs around its axis until it stabilized, bobbing slightly in the choppy waves. Cormac crawled to the upper side. The tree weighed scores of tons, and the branches acted as natural outriggers. The weight of a man, even a big man in iron armor, wasn't enough to significantly affect its balance.

He had been looking for Wulfhere ever since the wave struck. A hand reached out of the sea and clutched a branch ten feet down the trunk.

Cormac hopped to his feet, balancing on the log as he had often done on a ship's rail. Before he could reach out to help, Wulfhere's other hand, then his head and shoulders shot up from the sea. The Dane took a higher grip and threw himself astride the tree the way he mounted a horse when required to: accomplishing the task by main strength and awkwardness, but accomplishing it nonetheless.

"I was beginning to think you'd deserted me," Cormac said.

Wulfhere took the axe from under his belt and sank the blade deep in the soft wood between them. The helve gave the men something to grip with their hands besides the coarse bark.

"What do you mean, *me* desert?" he said. "I'm the captain, remember?"

Something raised itself from the nearby waves and dived again. Possibly a fish—really only a flash of movement in the corner of Cormac's eyes. But very likely a kronosaur or two had survived the collapse of the bubble world also.

He began to laugh. To survive *that*, and still to be swallowed whole by a lizard!

"It wasn't *that* funny," the Dane grumbled. "I don't suppose you've got anything to eat in that wallet of yours?"

"I don't—" the Gael began, but the words choked

as motion again glimmered in his peripheral vision. He jumped to his feet.

Wulfhere braced Cormac's stance with a hand on his knee. "If you go over," the Dane warned, "you're on your own."

"*I* don't have anything to eat," Cormac said, "but I'll bet *they* do. It's our ship, and a lubberly lot they look, too, with half the oars shipped and no sail set though the weather's turned fair."

He drew his sword and waved it overhead in a glittering steel arc. "Hey! you farmers. Hey!"

Wulfhere rose, stretched, and bellowed, "Ahoy the ship! Hakon, you lazy scut! Get a proper stroke going!"

The wallowing longship was a quarter mile away and the breeze was at best neutral. Despite the conditions, someone aboard the vessel heard their captain's shout. Crewmen waved. More of the oars hit the water.

Cormac and Wulfhere sat down again, waiting for the rescue neither of them had dared imagine. "Glad you decided to come along," the Dane said without looking at his companion. "Thanks."

Cormac gave a harsh, mocking laugh. "I wouldn't have missed it for the world," he said.

And he could almost believe the words as he spoke them, except that a vision of little Loughra veiled his sight of the returning long-ship.

TIGERS OF THE SEA

TIGERS OF THE SEA

"Tigers of the sea! Men with the hearts of wolves and thews of fire and steel! Feeders of ravens whose only joy lies in slaying and dying! Giants to whom the death-song of the sword is sweeter than the love-song of a girl!"

The tired eyes of King Gerinth were shadowed.

"This is no new tale to me; for a score of years such men have assailed my people like hunger-maddened wolves."

"Take a page from Caesar's book," answered Donal the minstrel as he lifted a wine goblet and drank deep. "Have we not read in the Roman books how he pitted wolf against wolf? Aye—that way he conquered our ancestors, who in their day were wolves also."

"And now they are more like sheep," murmured the king, a quiet bitterness in his voice. "In the years of the peace of Rome, our people forgot the arts of war. Now Rome has fallen and we fight for our lives— and cannot even protect our women."

Donal set down the goblet and leaned across the finely carved oak table.

"Wolf against wolf!" he cried. "You have told me— as well I knew!—that no warriors could be spared from the borders to search for your sister, the princess

Helen—even if you knew where she is to be found. Therefore, you must enlist the aid of other men—and these men I have just described to you are as superior in ferocity and barbarity to the savage Angles that assail us as the Angles themselves are superior to our softened peasantry."

"But would they serve under a Briton against their own blood?" demurred the king. "And would they keep faith with me?"

"They hate each other as much as we hate them both," answered the minstrel. "Moreover, you can promise them the reward—only when they return with the princess Helen."

"Tell me more of them," requested King Gerinth.

"Wulfhere the Skull-splitter, the chieftain, is a red-bearded giant like all his race. He is crafty in his way, but leads his Vikings mainly because of his fury in battle. He handles his heavy, long-shafted axe as lightly as if it were a toy, and with it he shatters the swords, shields, helmets and skulls of all who oppose him. When Wulfhere crashes through the ranks, stained with blood, his crimson beard bristling and his terrible eyes blazing and his great axe clotted with blood and brains, few there are who dare face him.

"But it is on his righthand man that Wulfhere depends for advise and council. That one is crafty as a serpent and is known to us Britons of old—for he is no Viking at all by birth, but a Gael of Erin, by name Cormac Mac Art, called *an Cliuin,* or the Wolf. Of old he led a band of Irish reivers and harried the coasts of the British Isles and Gaul and Spain—aye, and he preyed also on the Vikings themselves. But civil war broke up his band and he joined the forces of Wulfhere—they are Danes and dwell in a land south of the people who are called Norsemen.

"Cormac Mac Art has all the guile and reckless valor of his race. He is tall and rangy, a tiger where Wulfhere is a wild bull. His weapon is the sword, and his skill is incredible. The Vikings rely little on the art of fencing; their manner of fighting is to deliver mighty blows with the full sweep of their arms. Well, the Gael can deal a full arm blow with the best of them, but he favors the point. In a world where the old-time skill of the Roman swordsman is almost forgotten, Cormac Mac Art is well-nigh invincible. He is cool and deadly as the wolf for which he is named, yet at times, in the fury of battle, a madness comes upon him that transcends the frenzy of the Berserk. At such times he is more terrible than Wulfhere, and men who would face the Dane flee before the blood-lust of the Gael."

King Gerinth nodded. "And could you find these men for me?"

"Lord King, even now they are within reach. In a lonely bay on the western coast, in a little-frequented region, they have beached their dragon-ship and are making sure that it is fully sea-worthy before moving against the Angles. Wulfhere is no sea-king; he has but one ship—but so swiftly he moves and so fierce is his crew that the Angles, Jutes and Saxons fear him more than any of their other foes. He revels in battle. He will do as you wish him, if the reward is great enough."

"Promise him anything you will," answered Gerinth. "It is more than a princess of the realm that has been stolen—it is my little sister."

His fine, deeply-lined face was strangely tender as he spoke.

"Let me attend to it," said Donal, refilling his goblet. "I know where these Vikings are to be found. I can pass among them—but I tell you before I start that it will take your Majesty's word, from your own lips, to convince Cormac Mac Art of—anything! Those Western Celts are more wary than the Vikings themselves."

Again King Gerinth nodded. He knew that the

minstrel had walked strange paths and that though he was loquacious on most subjects, he was tight-lipped on others. Donal was blest or cursed with a strange and roving mind and his skill with the harp opened many doors to him that axes could not open. Where a warrior had died, Donal of the Harp walked unscathed. He knew well many fierce sea-kings who were but grim legends and myths to most of the people of Britain, but Gerinth had never had cause to doubt the minstrel's loyalty.

II

Wulfhere of the Danes fingered his crimson beard and scowled abstractedly. He was a giant; his breast muscles bulged like twin shields under his scale mail corselet. The horned helmet on his head added to his great height, and with his huge hand knotted about the long shaft of a great axe he made a picture of rampant barbarism not easily forgotten. But for all his evident savagery, the chief of the Danes seemed slightly bewildered and undecided. He turned and growled a question to a man who sat near.

This man was tall and rangy. He was big and powerful, and though he lacked the massive bulk of the Dane, he more than made up for it by the tigerish litheness that was apparent in his every move. He was dark, with a smooth-shaven face and square-cut black hair. He wore none of the golden armlets or ornaments of which the Vikings were so fond. His mail was of chain mesh and his helmet, which lay beside him, was crested with flowing horse-hair.

"Well, Cormac," growled the pirate chief, "what think you?"

Cormac Mac Art did not reply directly to his friend. His cold, narrow, grey eyes gazed full into the blue eyes of Donal the minstrel. Donal was a thin man of more than medium height. His wayward unruly hair was yellow. Now he bore neither harp nor sword and his dress was whimsically reminiscent of a court jester. His thin, patrician face was as inscrutable at the moment as the sinister, scarred features of the Gael.

"I trust you as much as I trust any man," said Cormac, "but I must have more than your mere word on the matter. How do I know that this is not some trick to send us on a wild goose chase, or mayhap into a nest of our enemies? We have business on the east coast of Britain—"

"The matter of which I speak will pay you better than the looting of some pirate's den," answered the minstrel. "If you will come with me, I will bring you to the man who may be able to convince you. But you must come alone, you and Wulfhere."

"A trap," grumbled the Dane. "Donal, I am disappointed in you—"

Cormac, looking deep into the minstrel's strange eyes, shook his head slowly.

"No, Wulfhere; if it be a trap, Donal too is duped and that I cannot believe."

"If you believe that," said Donal, "why can you not believe my mere word in regard to the other matter?"

"That is different," answered the reiver. "Here only my life and Wulfhere's is involved. The other concerns every member of our crew. It is my duty to them to require every proof. I do not think you lie; but you may have been lied to."

"Come, then, and I will bring you to one whom you will believe in spite of yourself."

Cormac rose from the great rock whereon he had been sitting and donned his helmet. Wulfhere, still grumbling and shaking his head, shouted an order to the Vikings who sat grouped about a small fire a short distance away, cooking a haunch of venison. Others were tossing dice in the sand, and others still working on the dragon-ship which was drawn up on the beach. Thick forest grew close about this cove, and that fact, coupled with the wild nature of the region, made it an ideal place for a pirate's rendezvous.

"All sea-worthy aud ship-shape," grumbled Wulfhere, referring to the galley. "On the morrow we could have sailed forth on the Viking path again—"

"Be at ease, Wulfhere," advised the Gael. "If Donal's man does not make matters sufficiently clear for our satisfaction, we have but to return and take the path."

"Aye—if we return."

"Why, Donal knew of our presence. Had he wished to betray us, he could have led a troop of Gerinth's horsemen upon us, or surrounded us with British bowmen. Donal, at least, I think, means to deal squarely with us as he has done in the past. It is the man behind Donal I mistrust."

The three had left the small bay behind them and now walked along in the shadow of the forest. The land tilted upward rapidly and soon the forest thinned out to straggling clumps and single gnarled oaks that grew between and among huge boulders—boulders broken as if in a Titan's play. The landscape was rugged and wild in the extreme. Then at last they rounded a cliff and saw a tall man, wrapped in a purple cloak, standing beneath a mountain oak. He was alone and Donal walked quickly toward him, beckoning his companions to follow. Cormac showed no sign of what he thought, but Wulfhere growled in his beard as he gripped the shaft of his axe and glanced suspiciously on all sides, as if expecting a horde of swordsmen to burst out of ambush. The three stopped before the silent man and Donal doffed his feathered cap. The man dropped his cloak and Cormac gave a low exclamation.

"By the blood of the gods! King Gerinth himself!"

He made no movement to kneel or to uncover his head, nor did Wulfhere. These wild rovers of the sea acknowledged the rule of no king. Their attitude was the respect accorded a fellow warrior; that was all. There was neither insolence nor deference in their manner, though Wulfhere's eyes did widen slightly as he gazed at the man whose keen brain and matchless valor had for years, and against terrific odds, stemmed the triumphant march of the Saxons to the Western sea.

The Dane saw a tall, slender man with a weary aristocratic face and kindly grey eyes. Only in his black hair was the Latin strain in his veins evident. Behind him lay the ages of a civilization now crumbled to the dust before the onstriding barbarians. He represented the last far-flung remnant of Rome's once mighty empire, struggling on the waves of barbarism which had engulfed the rest of that empire in one red inundation. Cormac, while possessing the true Gaelic antipathy for his Cymric kin in general, sensed the pathos and valor of this brave, vain struggle, and even Wulfhere, looking into the far-seeing eyes of the British king, felt a trifle awed. Here was a people, with their back to the wall, fighting grimly for their lives and at the same time vainly endeavoring to uphold the culture and ideals of an age already gone forever. The gods of Rome had faded under the ruthless heel of Goth and Vandal. Flaxen-haired savages reigned in the purple halls of the vanished Caesars. Only in this far-flung isle a little band of Romanized Celts clung to the traditions of yesterday.

"These are the warriors, your Majesty," said Donal, and Gerinth nodded and thanked him with the quiet courtesy of a born nobleman.

"They wish to hear again from your lips what I have told them," said the bard.

"My friends," said the king quietly, "I come to ask

your aid. My sister, the princess Helen, a girl of twenty years of age, has been stolen—how, or by whom, I do not know. She rode into the forest one morning attended only by her maid and a page, and she did not return. It was on one of those rare occasions when our coasts were peaceful; but when search parties were sent out, they found the page dead and horribly mangled in a small glade deep in the forest. The horses were found later, wandering loose, but of the princess Helen and her maid there was no trace. Nor was there ever a trace found of her, though we combed the kingdom from border to sea. Spies sent among the Angles and Saxons found no sign of her, and we at last decided that she had been taken captive and borne away by some wandering band of sea-farers who, roaming inland, had seized her and then taken to sea again.

"We are helpless to carry on such a search as must be necessary if she is to be found. We have no ships—the last remnant of the British fleet was destroyed in the sea-fight off Cornwall by the Saxons. And if we had ships, we could not spare the men to man them, not even for the princess Helen. The Angles press hard on our eastern borders and Cerdic's brood raven upon us from the south. In my extremity I appeal to you. I cannot tell you where to look for my sister. I cannot tell you how to recover her if found. I can only say: in the name of God, search the ends of the world for her, and if you find her, return with her and name your price."

Wulfhere glanced at Cormac as he always did in matters that required thought.

"Better that we set a price before we go," grunted the Gael.

"Then you agree?" cried the king, his fine face lighting.

"Not so fast," returned the wary Gael. "Let us first bargain. It is no easy task you set us: to comb the seas for a girl of whom nothing is known save that she was stolen. How if we search the oceans and return empty-handed?"

"Still I will reward you," answered the king. "I have gold in plenty. Would I could trade it for warriors— but I have Vortigern's example before me."

"If we go and bring back the princess, alive or dead," said Cormac, "you shall give us a hundred pounds of virgin gold, and ten pounds of gold for each man we lose on the voyage. If we do our best and cannot find the princess, you shall still give us ten pounds for every man slain in the search, but we will waive further reward. We are not Saxons, to haggle over money. Moreover, in either event you will allow us to overhaul our long ship in one of your bays, and furnish us with material enough to replace such equipment as may be damaged during the voyage. Is it agreed?"

"You have my word and my hand on it," answered the king, stretching out his arm, and as their hands met Cormac felt the nervous strength in the Briton's fingers.

"You sail at once?"

"As soon as we can return to the cove."

"I will accompany you," said Donal suddenly, "and there is another who would come also."

He whistled abruptly—and came nearer to sudden decapitation than he guessed; the sound was too much like a signal of attack to leave the wolf-like nerves of the sea-farers untouched. Cormac and Wulfhere, however, relaxed as a single man strode from the forest.

"This is Marcus, of a noble British house," said Donal, "the betrothed of the princess Helen. He too will accompany us if he may."

The young man was above medium height and well built. He was in full chain mail armor and wore the crested helmet of a legionary; a straight thrusting-sword was girt upon him. His eyes were grey, but his black hair and the faint olive-brown tint of his complexion showed that the warm blood of the South ran far more strongly in his veins than in those of his king. He was undeniably handsome, though now his face was shadowed with worry.

"I pray you will allow me to accompany you." He addressed himself to Wulfhere. "The game of war is not unknown to me—and waiting here in ignorance of the fate of my promised bride would be worse to me than death."

"Come if you will," growled Wulfhere. "It's like we'll need all the swords we can muster before the cruise is over. King Gerinth, have you no hint whatever of who took the princess?"

"None. We found only a single trace of anything out of the ordinary in the forests. Here it is."

The king drew from his garments a tiny object and passed it to the chieftain. Wulfhere stared, unenlightened, at the small, polished flint arrowhead which lay in his huge palm. Cormac took it and looked closely at it. His face was inscrutable but his cold eyes flickered momentarily. Then the Gael said a strange thing:

"I will not shave today, after all."

III

The fresh wind filled the sails of the dragon-ship and the rhythmic clack of many oars answered the deep-chested chant of the rowers. Cormac Mac Art, in full armor, the horse-hair of his helmet floating in the breeze, leaned on the rail of the poop-deck. Wulfhere banged his axe on the deal planking and roared an unnecessary order at the steersman.

"Cormac," said the huge Viking, "who is king of Britain?"

"Who is king of Hades when Pluto is away?" asked the Gael.

"Read me no runes from your knowledge of Roman myths," growled Wulfhere.

"Rome ruled Britain as Pluto rules Hades," answered Cormac. "Now Rome has fallen and the lesser demons are battling among themselves for mastery. Some eighty years ago the legions were withdrawn from Britain when Alaric and his Goths sacked the imperial city. Vortigern was king of Britain—or rather, made himself so when the Britons had to look to themselves for aid. He let the wolves in, himself, when he hired Hengist and Horsa and their Jutes to fight off the Picts, as you know. The Saxons and Angles poured in after them like a red wave and Vortigern fell. Britain is split into three Celtic kingdoms now, with the pirates holding all the eastern coast and slowly but surely forcing their way westward. The southern kingdom, Damnonia and the country extending to Caer Odun, is ruled over by Uther Pendragon. The middle kingdom, from Uther's lines to the foot of the Cumbrian Mountains, is held by Gerinth. North of his kingdom is the realm known by the Britons as Strath-Clyde—King Garth's domain. His people are the wildest of all the Britons, for many of them are tribes which were never fully conquered by Rome. Also, in the most westwardly tip of Damnonia and among the western mountains of Gerinth's land are barbaric tribes who never acknowledged Rome and do not now acknowledge any one of the three kings. The whole land is prey to robbers and bandits, and the three kings are not always at peace among themselves, owing to Uther's waywardness, which is tinged with madness, and to Garth's innate savagery. Were it not that Gerinth acts as a buffer between them, they would have been at each other's throats long ago.

"As it is they seldom act in concert for long. The Jutes, Angles and Saxons who assail them are forever at war among themselves also, as you know, but a never-ending supply streams across the Narrow Seas in their long, low galleys."

"That too I well know," growled the Dane, "having sent some score of those galleys to Midgaard. Some day my own people will come and take Britain from them."

"It is a land worth fighting for," responded the Gael. "What think you of the men we have shipped aboard?"

"Donal we know of old. He can tear the heart from my breast with his harp when he is so minded, or make me a boy again. And in a pinch we know he can wield a sword. As for the Roman—" so Wulfhere termed Marcus, "he has the look of a seasoned warrior."

"His ancestors were commanders of British legions for three centuries, and before that they trod the battlefields of Gaul and Italy with Caesar. It is but the remnant of Roman strategy lingering in the British knights that has enabled them to beat back the Saxons thus far. But, Wulfhere, what think you of my beard?" The Gael rubbed the bristly stubble that covered his face.

"I never saw you so unkempt before," grunted the Dane, "save when we had fled or fought for days so you could not be hacking at your face with a razor."

"It will hide my scars in a few days," grinned Cormac. "When I told you to head for Ara in Dalriadia, did naught occur to you?"

"Why, I assumed you would ask for news of the princess among the wild Scots there."

"And why did you suppose I would expect them to know?"

Wulfhere shrugged his shoulders. "I am done seeking to reason out your actions."

Cormac drew from his pouch the flint arrowhead. "In all the British Isles there is but one race who makes such points for their arrows. They are the Picts of Caledonia, who ruled these isles before the Celts came, in the age of stone. Even now they tip their arrows often with flint, as I learned when I fought under King Gol of Dalriadia. There was a time, soon after the legions left Britain, when the Picts ranged like wolves clear to the southeru coast. But the Jutes and Angles and Saxons drove them back into the heather country, and for so long has King Garth served as a buffer between them and Gerinth that he and his people have forgotten their ways."

"Then you think Picts stole the princess? But how did they—?"

"That is for me to learn; that's why we are heading for Ara. The Dalriadians and the Picts have been alternately fighting with each other and against each other for over a hundred years. Just now there is peace between them and the Scots are likely to know much of what goes on in the Dark Empire, as the Pictish kingdom is called—and dark it is, and strange. For these Picts come of an old, old race and their ways are beyond our ken."

"And we will capture a Scot and question him?"

Cormac shook his head. "I will go ashore and mingle with them; they are of my race and language."

"And when they recognize you," grunted Wulfhere, "they will hang you to the highest tree. They have no cause to love you. True, you fought under King Gol in your early youth, but since then you have raided Dalriadia's coasts more than once—not only with your Irish reivers, but with me, likewise."

"And that is why I am growing a beard, old sea-dragon," laughed the Gael.

IV

Night had fallen over the rugged western coast of Caledon. Eastward loomed against the stars the distant mountains; westward, the dark seas stretched away to uncharted gulfs and unknown shores. The *Raven* rode at anchor on the northern side of a wild and rugged promontory that ran out into the sea, hugging close those beetling cliffs. Under cover of darkness Cormac had steered her inshore, threading the treacherous reefs of that grim shore with a knowledge born of long experience. Cormac Mac Art was Erinborn, but all the isles of the Western Sea had been his stamping ground since the day he had been able to lift his first sword.

"And now," said Cormac, "I go ashore—alone."

"Let me go with you!" cried Marcus, eagerly, but the Gael shook his head.

"Your appearance and accent would betray us both. Nor can you either, Donal, for though I know the kings of the Scots have listened to your harp, you are the only one besides myself who knows this coast, and if I fail to return you must take her out."

The Gael's appearance was vastly altered. A thick, short beard masked his features, concealing his scars. He had laid aside his horse-hair crested helmet and his finely worked mail shirt, and had donned the round helmet and crude scale mail corselet of the Dalriadians. The arms of many nations were part of the *Raven*'s cargo.

"Well, old sea-wolf," said he with a wicked grin, as he prepared to lower himself over the rail, "you have said nothing, but I see a gleam in your eyes; do you also wish to accompany me? Surely the Dalriadians could have nothing but welcome for so kind a friend who has burnt their villages and sunk their hide-bottomed boats."

Wulfhere cursed him heartedly. "We sea-farers are so well loved by the Scots that my red beard alone would be enough to hang me. But even so, were I not captain of this ship, and bound by duty to it, I'd chance it rather than see you go into danger alone, and you such an empty-headed fool!"

Cormac laughed deeply. "Wait for me until dawn," he instructed, "and no longer."

Then, dropping from the after rail, he struck out for the shore, swimming strongly in spite of his mail and weapons. He swam along the base of the cliffs and presently found a shelving ledge from which a steep incline led upward. It might have taxed the agility of a mountain goat to have made the ascent there, but Cormac was not inclined to make the long circuit about the promontory. He climbed straight upward and, after a considerable strain of energy and skill, he gained the top of the cliffs and made his way along them to the point where they joined a steep ridge on the mainland. Down the southern slope of this he made his way toward the distant twinkle of fires that marked the Dalriadian town of Ara.

He had not taken half a dozen steps when a sound behind him brought him about, blade at the ready. A huge figure bulked dimly in the starlight.

"Hrut! What in the name of seven devils—"

"Wulfhere sent me after you," rumbled the big carle. "He feared harm might come to you."

Cormac was a man of irascible temper. He cursed Hrut and Wulfhere impartially. Hrut listened stolidly and Cormac knew the futility of arguing with him. The big Dane was a silent, moody creature whose mind had been slightly affected by a sword-cut on the head. But he was brave and loyal and his skill at wood-craft was second only to Cormac's.

"Come along," said Cormac, concluding his tirade, "but you cannot come into the village with me. You understand that you must hide outside the walls?"

The carle nodded, and motioning him to follow, Cormac took up his way at a steady trot. Hrut followed swiftly and silently as a ghost for all his bulk. Cormac went swiftly, for he would be crowded indeed to accomplish what he had set out to do and return to the dragon-ship by mid-day—but he went warily, for he expected momentarily to meet a party of warriors leaving or returning to the town. Yet luck was with him, and soon he crouched among the trees within arrow shot of the village.

"Hide here," he whispered to Hrut, "and on no account come any nearer the town. If you hear a brawl, wait until an hour before dawn; then, if you have heard naught from me, go back to Wulfhere. Do you understand?"

The usual nod was the answer and as Hrut faded back among the trees, Cormac went boldly toward the village.

Ara was build close to the shore of a small, land-locked bay and Cormac saw the crude hide coracles of the Dalriadians drawn up on the beach. In these they swept south in fierce raids on the Britons and Saxons, or crossed to Ulster for supplies and reinforcements. Ara was more of an army camp than a town, the real seat of Dalriadia lying some distance inland.

The village was not a particularly imposing place. Its few hundred wattle and mud huts were surrounded by a low wall of rough stones, but Cormac knew the temper of its inhabitants. What the Caledonian Gaels lacked in wealth and armament they made up in unquenchable ferocity. A hundred years of ceaseless conflict with Pict, Roman, Briton and Saxon had left them little opportunity to cultivate the natural seeds of civilization that was an heritage of their native land. The Gaels of Caledonia had gone backward a step; they were behind their Irish cousins in culture and artisanship, but they had not lost an iota of the Gaelic fighting fury.

Their ancestors had come from Ulahd into Caledonia, driven by a stronger tribe of the southern Irish. Cormac, born in what was later known as Connacht, was a son of these conquerors, and felt himself not only distinct from these transplanted Gaels, but from their cousins in northern Erin. Still, he had spent enough time among these people to deceive them, he felt.

He strode up to the crude gate and shouted for entrance before he was perceived by the guard, who were prone to be lax in their vigilance in the face of apparent quietude—a universal Celtic trait. A harsh voice ordered him to stand still, while a torch thrust above the gate shone its flickering light full on him. In its illumination Cormac could see, framed above the gate, fierce faces with unkempt beards and cold grey or blue eyes.

"Who are you?" one of the guards demanded.

"Partha Mac Othna, of Ulahd. I have come to take service under your chief, Eochaidh Mac Ailbe."

"Your garments are dripping wet."

"And they were not it would be a marvel," answered Cormac. "There was a boat load of us set sail from Ulahd this morning. On the way a Saxon sea-rover ran us down and all but I perished in the waves and the arrows the pirates rained upon us. I caught a piece of the broken mast and essayed to float."

"And what of the Saxon?"

"I saw the sails disappear southward. Mayhap they raid the Britons."

"How is it that the guard along the beach did not see you when you finally came ashore?"

"I made shore more than a mile to the south, and

glimpsing the lights through the trees, came here. I have been here aforetime and knew it to be Ara, whither I was bound."

"Let him in," growled one of the Dalriadians. "His tale rings true."

The clumsy gate swung open and Cormac entered the fortified camp of his hereditary foes. Fires blazed between the huts, and gathered close about the gate was the curious throng who had heard the guard challenge Cormac. Men, women and children partook of the wildness and savagery of their hard country. The women, splendidly built amazons with loose flowing hair, stared at him curiously, and dirty-faced, half-naked children peered at him from under shocks of tangled hair—and Cormac noted that each held a weapon of sorts. Brats scarcely able to toddle held a stone or a piece of wood. This symbolized the fierce life they led, when even the very babes had learned to snatch up a weapon at the first hint of alarm—aye, and to fight like wounded wildcats if need be. Cormac noted the fierceness of the people, their lean, hard savagery. No wonder Rome had never broken these people!

Some fifteen years had passed since Cormac had fought in the ranks of the ferocious warriors. He had no fear of being recognized by any of his former comrades. Nor, with his thick beard as a disguise, did he expect recognition as Wulfhere's comrade.

Cormac followed the warrior who led him toward the largest hut in the village. This, the pirate was sure, housed the chieftain and his folk. There was no elegance in Caledonia. King Gol's palace was a wattled hut. Cormac smiled to himself as he compared this village with the cities he had seen in his wanderings. Yet it was not walls and towers that made a city, he reflected, but the people within.

He was escorted into the great hut where a score of warriors were drinking from leather jacks about a crudely carved table. At the head sat the chief, known to Cormac of old, and at his elbow the inevitable minstrel—a characteristic of Celtic court life, however crude the court. Cormac involuntarily compared this skin-clad, shock-headed kern to the cultured and chivalrous Donal.

"Son of Ailbe," said Cormac's escort, "here is a weapon-man from Erin who wishes to take service under you."

"Who is your chief?" hiccupped Eochaidh, and Cormac saw that the Dalriadian was drunk.

"I am a free wanderer," answered the Wolf. "Aforetime I followed the bows of Donn Ruadh Mac Fin, *flaith na* Ulahd."

"Sit ye down and drink," ordered Eochaidh with an uncertain wave of his hairy hand. "Later I will talk with you."

No more attention was paid to Cormac, except the Scots made a place for him and a shock-headed gilly filled his cup with the fiery potheen so relished by the Gaels. The Wolf's ranging eye took in all the details of the scene, passed casually over the Dalriadian fighting-men and rested long on two men who sat almost opposite him. One of these Cormac knew—he was a renegade Norseman, Sigrel by name, who had found sanctuary among the foes of his race. Cormac's pulse quickened as he caught the evil eyes of the man fixed narrowly on him, but the sight of the man beside the Norseman made him forget Sigrel for the moment.

This man was short and strongly made. He was dark, much darker than Cormac himself, and from a face as immobile as an idol's, two black eyes glittered reptile-like. His square-cut black hair was caught back and confined by a narrow silver band about his temples, and he wore only a loin cloth and a broad leather girdle from which hung a short, barbed sword. A Pict! Cormac's heart leaped. He had intended drawing Eochaidh into conversation at once and, by the means of a tale he had already fabricated, to draw from him any information he might have of the whereabouts of the princess Helen. But the Dalriadian chief was too drunk for that now. He roared barbaric songs, pounded the board with his sword hilt in accompaniment to the wild strains of his minstrel's harp, and between times guzzled potheen at an astounding rate. All were drunk—all save Cormac and Sigrel, who furtively eyed the Gael over the rim of his goblet.

While Cormac racked his brain for a convincing way of drawing the Pict into conversation, the minstrel concluded one of his wild chants with a burst of sound and a rhyme that named Eochaidh Mac Ailbe "Wolf of Alba, greatest of raven-saters!"

The Pict reeled drunkenly to his feet, dashing his drinking-jack down on the board. The Picts habitually drank a smooth ale made from the heather blossoms. The fiery barley malt brewed by the Gaels maddened them. This particular Pict's brain was on fire. His face, no longer immobile, writhed demoniacally and his eyes glowed like coals of black fire.

"True, Eochaidh Mac Ailbe is a great warrior," he cried in his barbarous Gaelic, "but even he is not the greatest warrior in Caledonia. Who is greater than King Brogar, the Dark One, who rules the ancient throne of Pictdom? And next to him is Grulk! I am Grulk the Skull-cleaver! In my house in Grothga there is a mat woven of the scalps of Britons, Angles, Saxons—aye, and Scots!"

Cormac shrugged his shoulders in impatience. The drunken boastings of this savage would be likely to bring him a sword-thrust from the drink-fired Scots, that would cut off all chance of learning anything from him. But the Pict's next words electrified the Gael.

"Who of all Caledonia has taken a more beautiful woman from the southern Britons than Grulk?" he shouted, reeling and glaring. "There were five of us in the hide-bottomed boat the gale blew southward.

We went ashore in Gerinth's realm for fresh water, and there we came upon three Britons deep in the forest—one lad and two beautiful maidens. The boy showed fight, but I, Grulk, leaping upon his shoulders, bore him to earth and disembowelled him with my sword. The women we took into our boat and fled with them northward, and gained the coast of Caledonia, and took the women to Grothga!"

"Words—and empty words," sneered Cormac, leaning across the table. "There are no such women in Grothga now!"—taking a long chance.

The Pict howled like a wolf and fumbled drunkenly for his sword.

"When old Gonar, the high priest, looked on the face of the most finely dressed one—she who called herself Atalanta—he cried out that she was sacred to the moon god—that the symbol was upon her breast, though none but he could see. So he sent her, with the other, Marcia, to the Isle of Altars, in the Shetlands, in a long boat the Scots lent him, with fifteen warriors. The girl Atalanta is the daughter of a British nobleman and she will be acceptable in the eyes of Golka of the moon."

"How long since they departed for the Shetlands?" asked Cormac, as the Pict showed signs of making a quarrel of it.

"Three weeks; the night of the Nuptials of the Moon is not yet. But you said I lied—"

"Drink and forget it," growled a warrior, thrusting a brimming goblet at him. The Pict seized it with both hands and thrust his face into the liquor, guzzling ravenously, while the liquid slopped down on his bare chest. Cormac rose from his bench. He had learned all he wished to know, and he believed the Scots were too drunk to notice his casual departure from the hut. Outside it might be a different matter to get past the wall. But no sooner had he risen than another was on his feet. Sigrel, the renegade Viking, came around the table toward him.

"What, Partha," he said maliciously, "is your thirst so soon satisfied?"

Suddenly he thrust out a hand and pushed back the Gael's helmet from his brows. Cormac angrily struck his hand away, and Sigrel leaped back with a yell of ferocious triumph.

"Eochaidh! Men of Caledonia! A thief and a liar is among you!"

The drunken warriors gaped stupidly.

"This is Cormac *an Cliuin*," shouted Sigrel, reaching for his sword, "Cormac Mac Art, comrade of Wulfhere the Viking!"

Cormac moved with the volcanic quickness of a wounded tiger. Steel flashed in the flickering torchlight and Sigrel's head rolled grinning beneath the feet of the astonished revelers. A single bound carried the reiver to the door and he vanished while the Scots were struggling to their feet, roaring bewilderedly and tugging at their swords.

In an instant the whole village was in an uproar. Men had seen Cormac leap from the chief's hut with his red-stained sword in his hand and they gave chase without asking the reason for his flight. The partially sobered feasters came tumbling out of the hut yelling and cursing, and when they shouted the real identity of their erstwhile guest a thunderous roar of rage went up and the whole village joined vengefully in the chase.

Cormac, weaving in and out among the huts like a flying shadow, came on an unguarded point of the wall and, without slackening his headlong gait, cleared the low barrier with a bound and raced toward the forest. A quick glance over his shoulder showed him that his escape had been seen. Warriors were swarming over the wall, weapons in their hands.

It was some distance to the first thick tangle of

trees. Cormac took it full speed, running low and momentarily expecting an arrow between his shoulders. But the Dalriadians had no skill at archery and he reached the fringe of forest unscathed.

He had outfooted the fleet Caledonians, all save one who had outdistanced his fellows by a hundred yards and was now close upon the reiver's heels. Cormac wheeled to dispose of this single foe, and even as he turned a stone rolled under his foot and flung him to his knee. He flung up his blade to block the sword that hovered over him like the shadow of Doom—but before it could fall, a giant shape catapulted from the trees, a heavy sword crashed down, and the Scot fell limply across Cormac, his skull shattered.

The Gael flung off the corpse and leaped to his feet. The yelling pursuers were close now, and Hrut, snarling like a wild beast, faced them—but Cormac seized his wrist and dragged him back among the trees. The next instant they were fleeing in the direction from which they had first come to Ara, ducking and dodging among the trees.

Behind them, and presently on either side, they heard the crashing of men through the underbrush, and savage yells. Hundreds of warriors had joined in the hunt of their arch-enemy. Cormac and Hrut slackened their speed and went warily, keeping in the deep shadows, flitting from tree to tree, now lying prone in the bushes to let a band of searchers go by. They had progressed some little distance when Cormac was galvanized by the deep baying of hounds far behind them.

"We are ahead of our pursuers now, I think," muttered the Gael. "We might make a dash of it and gain the ridge and from thence the promontory and the ship. But they have loosed the wolfhounds on our trail and if we take that way, we will lead them and the warriors straight to Wulfhere's ship. There are enough of them to swim out and board her and take her by storm. We must swim for it."

Cormac turned westward, almost at right-angles to the course they had been following, and they quickened their pace recklessly—and emerging into a small glade ran full into three Dalriadians who assailed them with yells. Evidently they had not been ahead of their hunters as far as Cormac had thought, and the Gael, hurling himself fiercely into the fray, knew that the fight must be short or else the sound would bring scores of warriors hastening to the spot.

One of the Scots engaged Cormac while the other two fell upon the giant Hrut. A buckler turned Cormac's first vicious thrust and the Dalriadian's sword beat down on his helmet, biting through the metal and into the scalp beneath. But before the warrior could strike again, Cormac's sword cut his left leg from under him, through the knee, and as he crumpled another stroke shore through his neck cords.

In the meantime Hrut had killed one of his opponents with a bear-like stroke that rended the upflung shield as though it had been paper and crushed the skull it sought to guard, and as Cormac turned to aid him, the remaining foe leaped in with the desperate recklessness of a dying wolf, and it seemed to the Gael that his stabbing sword sank half way to the hilt in the Dane's mighty bosom. But Hrut gripped the Scot's throat in his huge left hand, thrust him away and struck a blow that shore through corselet and ribs and left the broken blade wedged in the dead man's spinal column.

"Are you hurt badly, Hrut?" Cormac was at his side, striving to undo the Dane's rent corselet so that he might staunch the flow of blood. But the carle pushed him away.

"A scratch," he said thickly. "I've broken my sword—let us haste."

Cormac cast a doubtful look at his companion, then

turned and hurried on in the direction they had been following. Seeing that Hrut followed with apparent ease, and hearing the baying of the hounds grow nearer, Cormac increased his gait until the two were running fleetly through the midnight forest. At length they heard the lapping of the sea, and even as Hrut's breathing grew heavy and labored they emerged upon a steep rocky shore, where the trees overhung the water. To the north, jutting out into the sea could be seen the vague bulk of the promontory behind which lay the *Raven*. Three miles of rugged coast lay between the promontory and the bay of Ara. Cormac and Hrut were at a point a little over halfway between, and slightly nearer the promontory than the bay.

"We swim from here," growled Cormac, "and it's a long swim to Wulfhere's ship, around the end of the promontory—for the cliffs are too steep to climb on this side—but we can make it and the hounds can't follow our tracks in the water—what in the name of gods—!"

Hrut had reeled and pitched headlong down the steep bank, his hands trailing in the water. Cormac reached him instantly and turned him on his back; but the Dane's fierce face was set in death. Cormac tore open his corselet and felt beneath it for an instant, then withdrew his hand and swore in amazement at the vitality that had enabled the carle to run for nearly half a mile with that terrible wound beneath his heart. The Gael hesitated; then to his ears came the deep baying of the hounds. With a bitter curse he tore off his helmet and corselet and threw them aside, kicking off his sandals. Drawing his sword belt up another notch, he waded out into the water and then struck out strongly.

In the darkness before dawn Wulfhere, pacing the deck of his dragon-ship, heard a faint sound that was not the lapping of the waves against the hull or the cliffs. With a quick word to his comrades, the Dane stepped to the rail and peered over. Marcus and Donal pressed close behind him, and presently saw a ghostly figure clamber out of the water and up the side. Cormac Mac Art, blood-stained and half naked, clambered over the rail and snarled:

"Out oars, wolves, and pull for the open sea, before we have half a thousand Dalriadians on our backs! And head her prow for the Shetlands—the Picts have taken Gerinth's sister there."

"Where's Hrut?" rumbled Wulfhere, as Cormac started toward the sweep-head.

"Drive a brass nail into the main-mast," snarled the Gael. "Gerinth owes us ten pounds already."

The bitterness in his eyes belied the harsh callousness of his words.

V

Marcus paced the deck of the dragon-ship. The wind filled the sails and the long ash oars of the rowers sent the long, lean craft hurtling through the water, but to the impatient Briton it seemed that they moved at a snail's pace.

"But why did the Pict call her Atalanta?" he cried, turning to Cormac. "True, her maid was named Marcia—but we have no real proof that the woman with her is the princess Helen."

"We have all the proof in the world," answered the Gael. "Do you think the princess would admit her true identity to her abductors? If they knew they held Gerinth's sister, they would have half his kingdom as ransom."

"But what did the Pict mean by the Nuptials of the Moon?"

Wulfhere looked at Cormac and Cormac started to speak, shot a quick glance at Marcus and hesitated.

"Tell him," nodded Donal. "He must know eventually."

"The Picts worship strange and abhorrent gods," said the Gael, "as is well known to we who roam the sea, eh Wulfhere?"

"Right," growled the giant. "Many a Viking has died on their altar stones."

"One of their gods is Golka of the Moon. Every so often they present a captured virgin of high rank to him. On a strange, lonely isle in the Shetlands stands a grim black altar, surrounded by columns of stone, such as you have seen at Stonehenge. On that altar, when the moon is full, the girl is sacrificed to Golka."

Marcus shuddered; his nails bit into his palms.

"Gods of Rome, can such things be?"

"Rome has fallen," grunted the Skull-splitter. "Her gods are dead. They will not aid us. But fear not—" he lifted his gleaming, keen-edged axe, "here is that which will aid us. Let me lead my wolves into the stone circle and we will give Golka such a blood-sacrifice as he has never dreamed of!"

"Sail on the port bow!" came the sudden shout of the look-out in the cross-trees. Wulfhere wheeled suddenly, beard bristling. A few moments later all on board could make out the long, low lines of the strange craft.

"A dragon-ship," swore Cormac, "and making full speed with oar and sail—she means to cut across our bows, Wulfhere."

The chieftain swore, his cold blue eyes beginning to blaze. His whole body quivered with eagerness and a new roaring note came into the voice that bellowed commands to his crew.

"By the bones of Thor, he must be a fool! But we'll give him his fill!"

Marcus caught the Dane's mighty arm and swung him about.

"Our mission is not to fight every sea-thief we meet," the young Briton cried angrily. "You were engaged to search for the princess Helen; we must not jeopardize this expedition. Now we have at last a clue; will you throw away our chances merely to glut your foolish lust for battle?"

Wulfhere's eyes flamed.

"This to me on my own deck?" he roared. "I'll not show my stern to any rover for Gerinth and all his gold! If it's fight he wants, it's fight he'll get."

"The lad's right, Wulfhere," said Cormac quietly, "but by the blood of the gods we'll have to run for it, for yon ship is aimed straight for us and I see a running about on the deck that can mean naught but preparation for a sea-fight."

"And run we cannot," said Wulfhere in deep satisfaction, "for I know her—that ship is Rudd Thorwald's *Fire-Woman*, and he is my life-long enemy. She is as fleet as the *Raven* and if we flee we will have her hanging on our stern all the way to the Shetlands. We must fight."

"Then let us make it short and desperate," snapped Cormac, scowling. "There's scant use in trying to ram her; run alongside and we'll take her by storm."

"I was born in a sea-fight, and I sank dragon-ships before I ever saw you," roared Wulfhere. "Take the sweep-head." He turned to Marcus. "Hast ever been in a sea-brawl, youngster?"

"No, but if I fail to go further than you can lead, hang me to your dragon-beak!" snapped the angered Briton.

Wulfhere's cold eyes glinted in amused appreciation as he turned away.

There was little maneuvering of ships in that primitive

age. The Vikings attained the sea-craft they had in a later day. The long, low serpents of the sea drove straight for each other, while warriors lined the sides of each, yelling and clashing sword on shield.

Marcus, leaning on the rail, glanced at the wolfish warriors beside and below him, and glanced across the intervening waves at the fierce, light-eyed, yellow-bearded Vikings who lined the sides of the opposing galley—Jutes they were, and hereditary enemies of the red-maned Danes. The young Briton shuddered involuntarily, not from fear but because of the innate, ruthless savagery of the scene, as a man might shudder at a pack of ravening wolves, without fearing them.

And now there came a giant twanging of bowstrings and a rain of death leaped through the air. Here the Danes had the advantage; they were the bowmen of the North Sea. The Jutes, like their Saxon cousins, knew little of archery. Arrows came whistling back, but their flight lacked the deadly accuracy of the Danish shafts. Marcus saw men go down in windrows aboard the Juttish craft, while the rest crouched behind the shields that lined the sides. The three men at the sweep-head fell and the long sweep swung in a wide, erratic arc; the gailey lost way and Marcus saw a blond giant he instinctively knew to be Rudd Thorwald himself leap to the sweep-head. Arrows rattled off his mail like hailstones, and then the two craft ran alongside with a rending and crashing of oars and a grinding of timbers.

The wolf-yell of the Vikings split the skies and in an instant all was a red chaos. The grappling hooks bit in, gripping keel to keel. Shields locked, the double line writhed and rocked as each crew sought to beat the other back from its bulwarks and gain the opposing deck. Marcus, thrusting and parrying with a wild-eyed giant across the rails, saw in a quick glance over his foe's shoulder Rudd Thorwald rushing from the sweep-head to the rail. Then his straight sword was through the Jute's throat and he flung one leg over the rail. But before he could leap into the other ship, another howling devil was hacking and hewing at him, and only a shield suddenly flung above his head saved his life. It was Donal the minstrel who had come to his aid.

Toward the waist of the ship, Wulfhere surged on through the fray and one mighty sweep of his axe cleared a space for him for an instant. In that instant he was over the rail on the deck of the *Fire-Woman* and Cormac, Thorfinn, Edric and Snorri were close behind him. Snorri died the moment his feet touched the *Fire-Woman's* deck and a second later a Juttish axe split Edric's skull, but already the Danes were pouring through the breach made in the lines of the defenders and in a moment the Jutes were fighting with their backs to the wall.

On the blood-slippery deck the two Viking chieftains met. Wulfhere's axe hewed the shaft of Rudd Thorwald's spear in twain, but before the Dane could strike again, the Jute snatched a sword from a dying hand and the edge bit through Wulfhere's corselet over his ribs. In an instant the Skull-splitter's mail was dyed red, but with a mad roar he swung his axe in a two-handed stroke that rent Rudd Thorwald's armor like paper and cleft through shoulder bone and spine. The Juttish chief fell dead in a red welter of blood and the Juttish warriors, disheartened, fell back, fighting desperately.

The Danes yelled with fierce delight. But the battle was not over. The Jutes, knowing there was no mercy for the losers of a sea-fight, battled stubbornly. Marcus was in the thick of it, with Donal close at his side. A strange madness had gripped the young Briton. To his mind, distorted momentarily by the fury of the fray, it seemed that these Jutes were holding him back from Helen. They stood in his way and while he and his comrades wasted time with them, Helen might be in desperate need of rescue. A red haze burned before Marcus' eyes and his sword wove a web of death in front of him. A huge Jute dented his shield with a sweeping axe-head and Marcus flung his shield away, ripping the warrior open with the other hand.

"By the blood of the gods," Cormac rasped, "I never heard before that Romans went berserk, but—"

Marcus had forced his way over the corpse-littered benches to the poop. A sword battered down on his helm as he leaped upward, but he paid no heed; even as he thrust mechanically, his eyes fell on a strangely incongruous ornament suspended by a slender, golden chain from the Jute's bull neck. On the end of that chain, glittering against his broad, mailed chest, hung a tiny jewel—a single ruby carved in the symbol of the acanthus. Marcus cried out like a man with a death wound under his heart and like a madman plunged in blindly, scarcely knowing what he did. He felt his blade sink deep and the force of his charge hurled him to the poop deck on top of his victim.

Struggling to his knees, oblivious to the hell of battle about him, Marcus tore the jewel from the pirate's neck and pressed it to his lips. Then he gripped the Jute's shoulders fiercely.

"Quick!" he cried in the tongue of the Angles, which the Jutes understood. "Tell me, before I rend the heart from your breast, whence you got this gem!"

The Jute's eyes were already glazing. He was past acting on his own initiative. He heard an insistent voice questioning him, and answered dully, scarcely knowing that he did so: "From one of the girls we took . . . from the . . . Pictish boat."

Marcus shook him, frantic with a sudden agony. "What of them? Where are they?"

Cormac, seeing something was forward, had broken from the fight and now bent, with Donal, over the dying pirate.

"We . . . sold . . . them," muttered the Jute in a fading whisper, "to . . . Thorleif Hordi's son . . . at . . ."

His head fell back; the voice ceased.

Marcus looked up at Donal with pain-haunted eyes.

"Look, Donal," he cried, holding up the chain with the ruby pendant. "See? It is Helen's! I myself gave it to her—she and Marcia were on this very ship— but now—who is this Thorleif Hordi's son?"

"Easy to say," broke in Cormac. "He is a Norse reiver who has established himself in the Hebrides. Be of good cheer, young sir; Helen is better off in the hands of the Vikings than in those of the Pictish savages of the Hjaltlands."

"But surely we must waste no time now!" cried Marcus. "The gods have cast this knowledge into our hands; if we tarry we may again be put upon a false scent!"

Wulfhere and his Danes had cleared the poop and waist, but on the after deck the survivors still stubbornly contended with their conquerors. There was scant mercy shown in a sea-fight of that age. Had the Jutes been victorious they would have spared none; nor did they expect or ask for mercy.

Cormac made his way through the waist of the ship where dead and dying lay heaped, and struggled his way through the yelling Danes to where Wulfhere stood plying his dripping axe. By main force he tore the Skull-splitter from his prey and jerked him about.

"Have done, old wolf," he growled. "The fight is won; Rudd Thorwald is dead. Would you waste steel on these miserable carles?"

"I leave this ship when no Jute remains alive!" thundered the battle-maddened Dane. Cormac laughed grimly.

"Have done! Bigger game is afoot! These Jutes will drink blood before you slaughter them all and we will need every man before the faring is over. From the lips of a dying Jute we have heard it—the princess is in the steading of Thorleif Hordi's son, in the Hebrides."

Wulfhere's beard bristled with ferocious joy. So many were his foes that it was hard to name a Viking farer with whom he had no feud.

"Is it so? Then, ho, wolves—leave the rest of these sea-rats to drown or swim as they will! We go to burn Thorleif Hordi's son's skalli over his head!"

Slowly, by words and blows, he beat his raging Danes off and, marshalling them together, drove them over the gunwales into their own ship. The bleeding, battle-weary Jutes watched them go, leaning on their reddened weapons in sullen silence. The toll taken had been terrific, but by far the greater loss aboard the *Fire-Woman*. From stem to stern dead men wallowed among the broken benches in a welter of crimson.

"Ho, rats!" Wulfhere shouted, as his Vikings cast off and the oars of the *Raven* began to ply, "I leave you your blood-gutted craft and the carrion that was Rudd Thorwald. Make the best you can of them and thank the gods that I spared your lives!"

The losers harkened in sullen silence, answering only with black scowls, all save one—a lean, wolfish figure of a warrior, who brandished a notched and bloody axe and shouted: "Mayhap you will curse the gods some day, Skull-splitter, because you spared Halfgar Wolf's-tooth!"

It was a name, in sooth, that Wulfhere had cause to remember well in later days. But now the chief merely roared in laughter, though Cormac frowned.

"It is a foolish thing to taunt beaten men, Wulfhere," said he. "But you have a nasty cut across your ribs. Let me see to it."

Marcus turned away with the gem that Helen had worn. The flood of savagery during the last few hours left him dazed and weary. But he had discovered strange, dark deeps in his own soul. A few minutes of fierce sword-play on the gunwales of a sea-rover had sufficed to bridge the gap of three centuries. Coolness in action, a characteristic drilled into his forebears by countless Roman officers, and inherited by him, had been swept away in an instant before the wild, old Celtic fury before which Caesar had staggered on the Ceanntish beaches. For a few mad moments he had been one with the wild men about him. The shadows of Rome were fading; was he, too, like all the world, reverting to the nature of his British ancestors, blood-brothers in savagery to Wulfhere Skull-splitter?

VI

"It is not far from here to Kaldjorn where Thorleif Hordi's son has built his steading," said Cormac, glancing abstractedly at the mast where now sixteen brass nails gleamed dully.

The Norse were already establishing themselves in the Hebrides, the Orkneys and the Shetlands. Later these movements would become permanent colonizations; at this time, however, their steadings were merely pirate camps.

"The Sudeyar lie to the east, just out of sight over the sea-rim," Cormac continued. "We must resort to craft again. Thorleif Hordi's son has four long ships and three hundred carles. We have one ship and less than eighty men. We cannot do as Wulfhere wishes: go ashore and burn Thorleif's skalli—and he will not be likely to give up such a prize as the princess Helen without a battle.

"This is what I suggest: Thorleif's steading is on the east side of the isle of Kaldjorn, which luckily is a small one. We will draw in under cover of night, on the west side. There are high cliffs there and the ship should be safe from detection for a time, since none of Thorleif's folk have any reason to wander about on the western part of the island. Then I will go ashore and seek to steal the princess."

Wulfhere laughed. "You will find it a more difficult matter to hoax the Norse than you did the Scots. Your locks will brand you as a Gael and they will cut the blood-eagle in your back."

"I will creep among them like a serpent and they will know naught of my coming," answered the Gael. "Your Norseman is a very dullard when it comes to stealth, and easy to deceive."

"I will go with you," broke in Marcus. "This time I will not be denied."

"While I must gnaw my thumb on the west side of the isle," grumbled Wulfhere enviously.

"Wait," said Donal. "I have a better plan, Cormac."

"This plan, that plan," Wulfhere said. "Numbers mean little if we take Thorleif unaware. I think we should attack."

"If you *thought*, then you'd say nothing of the sort," Cormac said with a sharpness no other would have dared use on the Danish chief. "We'll have fighting enough, without we bring three hundred reivers down on us because Thorleif's dogs barked a warning that his swordsmen were sober enough to wake to. Donal, what have you to say?"

"Dogs might bark at a serpent as well, Cormac," the harper said. "But if they barked at a British thrall, who among the Vikings would care? There will be as many slaves as Norsemen on Kaldjorn. One more Briton, wearing rough clothes and speaking only the slave tongue, will go unnoticed. I can slip into the steading as a thrall among thralls, gathering the knowledge we will need if we're to have a real chance of retrieving Helen."

"The slaves will know you," Cormac said. "Are you so sure that none of them will betray you if you go openly among them? Not all the captives will be from Gerinth's lands, and even if they were—Gerinth would be a saint, not a king, if he were loved by all his subjects."

"I put my trust not in love of Gerinth," said Donal, "but in the hatred decent folk, ripped from their farms or hamlets, have for the barbarians who enslaved them. Though Thorlief's thralls will not know why I'm on Kaldjorn, they'll know I mean no good service to their iron-handed captor."

Cormac, Wulfhere and Marcus looked at one another. Marcus bit his lip but did not speak. Cormac laughed harshly and clapped Donal on the shoulder. "All right, harper," he said. "We'll set you ashore on the west side of the island. Further plans will await your return."

"But if you tell us Thorlief's dogs sleep sound of a night . . ." said Wulfhere. The Dane balanced his great axe on the tip his right index finger, ashwood helve exactly counterweighting the hooked steel head. "Then I've a plan sufficient to our task."

The sea breeze, cold and ceaseless, blew bone-deep through Cormac and the small band who waited with him in darkness. Fifty of the *Raven*'s crew slept at their oar benches, ready to push off if danger threatened. The chiefs and ten men only waited to greet Donal or guard him home if Norsemen pursued him.

The wind skirled around the standing stones, a trio of inward-leaning posts that were the only marker on the bleak upland moor forming the interior of Kaldjorn. Donal had said the stones were called the Whispering Chieftains. The rasp of the wind across granite sounded to Cormac's ears like a secret conclave.

"He may not return tonight," Marcus said miserably,

hugging his thick wool cloak tighter about his armored chest.

"Donal has this and one other remaining of the three days we agreed with him," Cormac said. "Impatience has lost more battles than cowardice, lad."

"Yes, well," Wulfhere said, absently polishing his axe on his sheepskin vest. "It's a good plan to let them come within arm's reach, anyway."

"The trouble is that it's Thorlief who holds her," Marcus said. His eyes were on the moorland, empty except for the sedges and heather which grew no higher than a man's knee. "Two years ago Thorlief's brother Rollo raided us. A troop of our horse caught the Vikings at a river ford as they were returning burdened with plunder. We killed them all."

Cormac turned his gaze on the Roman. "I'd heard that story," he said. "Thorlief and his brother were twins, though Rollo was stocky and blond and Thorlief himself tall and nigh as dark as me."

"Thorlief sent his nephew Rolf, Rollo's son, to buy back the corpse for their pagan rites," Marcus continued. "He arrived weeks too late. We'd stripped the bodies and dumped them in the river as soon as the battle was over."

Wulfhere shook his head in amusement. "No mourners but the eels who ate their flesh, hey?" he said. "Well, that's the monument I'd have given Rollo had I killed him. And there'll be nothing better for Thorlief, if the gods grant my longings."

"You said, 'we stripped the bodies,'" Cormac said. "Is that we, Gerinth's men, or—?"

"My men and I!" Marcus snapped. "Well, what were we to do? Raise a marble tomb to the butchers who'd been raping and slaughtering our people?"

"What's done is done," Cormac said. "But Helen was wise to take a false name."

Wulfhere chuckled. "Aye," he said. "If Thorlief

learns who she really is, the best she can hope for is to entertain every man in the steading before daybreak."

"Hsst!" said Cormac. "We've a visitor."

The night was moonless and the wind blew from the sea to their backs. The oncoming figure had come within fifty yards of the Whispering Chieftains before even the Gael's preternaturally sharp senses had spotted him. A single figure, hunched against the wind. A blotch against the greater blotch of the moor . . .

Swords skritched as they slid from their sheaths.

The figure paused. "I come as a friend," called Donal's mellifluous voice. "If you like, I'll wait here while you advance to me."

"Come in on your own legs, Donal," Cormac replied. "What news from the steading?"

"News a-plenty," said the minstrel as he joined the reivers. "Let's go to the *Raven* and get under way while I tell you."

Donal wore a hooded brown cape over a jerkin and breeks of gray wool for his reconnaissance. He'd lost one of his cowhide moccasins in his scramble across the moor to the rendezvous, and his legs to the knees were covered with cold mud.

"Wait!" said Wulfhere. "Are you pursued, man?"

"I think not," Donal said. He took a deep breath. His jerkin was sweaty from exertion despite the chill wind. Crossing the island in haste on a moonless night was a brutal task, even for a man not burdened by weapons and armor.

"Then we'll wait here the while," Wulfhere said. "It lacks two hours of dawn, and we'll lose more time by launching the ship before first light."

"Aye," Cormac agreed, handing Donal a skin of British beer. "Time and a man or two, like enough, rolled under by the hull. Tell us your news, minstrel."

Donal drank deeply before he lowered the skin with a grateful expression. "Atalanta is indeed being held at Thorlief's stead," the minstel said. His breathing adapted naturally to the rhythms of the tale. "She's accompanied at all times by the Vikings' women and by two armed men as well. At night she's kept in a close-bed barred from the outside. Thorlief takes no chances with a prize he's sure will bring him great ransom."

"They know who she is, then?" Wulfhere asked with a frown.

"Nay," said Donal. "Atalanta has told him she's the daughter of Artorius, Uther's master of horse—his military chief. Envoys will go south to Damnonia in a few days."

"And when they return with news the tale was a lie," Marcus groaned, "Thorlief will torture Helen's maid and perhaps Helen herself to learn the truth. We must rescue her!"

"If she's locked in a close-bed, we dare not make a night attack," Cormac said grimly. "Fire is the only weapon we have to even the odds against us, and the prize would burn among the swordsmen guarding her."

"Thorlief will not torture Atalanta's maid," Donal said, "for Rolf Rollo's son, Thorlief's nephew, has stolen away that girl in a yawl the steading used to communicate with the mainland. The night before last they went off, though all the folk wonder why they should have done so. Rolf is Thorlief's nearest kin. No one would have objected had the boy claimed the servant openly to warm his bed."

Unconscious of what he was doing, Donal held the beer skin in the crook of his left arm as if it were a harp. Only moments after running across the nighted moor, Donal had donned his minstrel's persona again. He was entertaining rather than merely informing.

"We can capture Rolf!" Marcus said. "Offer to trade him to his uncle for Helen, a life for a life. *That* ransom Thorlief won't refuse, even for Gerinth's daughter!"

"Ah, but we cannot do that," Donal said with a lilt in his voice, "because Thorlief doesn't hold Helen prisoner."

"You said—" Marcus blurted.

Cormac took Donal's chin between the thumb and forefinger of his left hand. He turned the minstrel to face him squarely. "Thorlief holds Marcia prisoner, wearing her mistress' clothing and such jewelry as previous captors left her," the Gael said. "That is so, isn't it, minstrel?"

He released Donal.

"Aye," the minstrel said, massaging his chin though the Gael's grip had only hinted at the strength of the fingers that controlled Cormac's shield in battle. In a chastened voice Donal added, "I would have told you in a moment."

"Next time keep a sense of proportion about when the burden of a tale might be of more importance than the artistry of its telling," Cormac said. "But in all, a bold scheme well-executed, Donal. You honor us by your comradeship."

"But why?" said Marcus. "That Rolf would recognize Helen from his embassy two years ago, that's likely enough. Indeed, I feared it from the first. But why would Rolf take the princess off by himself rather than denouncing her to the company?"

Cormac shrugged. It still an hour of dawn, but the eastern sky was vaguely paler than that to the west. "Let's make our way back to the ship," he said. "There'll be light enough by the time we're to the narrow portion of the descent. The less time we lose, the better."

The party moved off. Donal said to his fellow Briton, "Gold outweighs blood to some men of every race, Marcus. Rolf knew his uncle would never consent to ransoming Gerinth's sister. The boy can use the gold he receives for Helen to set up as a sea-king in his own right, rather than merely remain a sea-king's nephew."

Cormac waved Donal toward the hawser hung to ease the descent of the cliff. He heard the *sring-THOONK!* of a heavy blow behind them.

The Gael's sword was out in a dazzling arc of star-light along the edge. "Wulfhere!" he called. "Wul—"

The huge Dane ambled toward them from the Whispering Chieftains fifty yards away. He'd sheltered there unnoticed when the remainder of the party left. He held his axe at the balance in his right hand and wiped the blade with a swatch of cloth ripped from a jerkin.

"One of the carles followed the minstrel from the steading after all," Wulfhere said with satisfaction. "It would have been a pity to visit Thorlief and not give my axe a drink."

VII

The oar benches were manned as fully as previous losses allowed, but only four men astern and the two nearest Cormac in the prow kept the slow stroke as the *Raven* coasted the wooded shore.

"Shall we put in?" Wulfhere called from the steering oar.

The creek piercing the low corniche would be a torrent in spring when snow melting from the uplands north of the Wall of Severus fed the freshets, but the present current was so feeble that reeds grew out from either bank to nearly midstream. There was no sign of the yawl's passage, though with luck and skill Rolf might have slid his slight craft up the channel without grinding the reeds under.

"No, we can't risk—" Cormac began. His hawk-sharp gaze saw the gleam of bleached fabric caught in an eddy where the stream kinked into the trees. "Yes, by the seven devils!" he said. "They must have camped here last night. Put in, but easily. We'll be lucky not to scrape half our keel away on the bar."

The starboard oarsmen stroked gently forward while their fellows to port backed water, bringing the dragon-ship around in her own length. At Wulfhere's command the bow oarsmen trotted quickly sternward, lifting the prow as the vessel slipped into the creek. They ran forward again, joined by half the crewmen from the stern, when the midpoint of the keel had passed the gravel bar that springtime floods deposited. The *Raven* lurched with a grate of planking, but the contact wasn't violent enough to endanger the hull.

As the bow slapped down, Cormac leaned far outboard and snagged the trail of cloth with the point of a spear. It was a linen girdle embroidered in a floral pattern with no great skill. The item was of civilized manufacture—no product of these Pictish glens, and not of high enough quality to have been imported to clothe the wife of a skin-clad chieftain. It was the sort of garment that Helen's maid Marcia might well have worn. . . .

"Put into the bank!" Cormac ordered as the longship's bow passed the kink in the stream's course. "We've found them!"

A single-masted yawl, clinker-built of overlapping planks in Scandinavian fashion, had been drawn as far up the shingle bank as a strong man could manage alone. In the boat's lee were bedding and the remains of a fire, now too cold to smoke.

Rolf and his captive *had* been here. The reason they were gone—had fled—lay on the other side of the yawl: a Pictish warrior, split halfway through the chest by a Viking broadsword. Faint through the screening forest, Cormac heard the clash of weapons and the despairing cry of a soul ripped from its fleshly home.

"Come!" the Gael cried. "A dozen men to stay with the ship. The rest with me or all our risk till now has been bootless!"

Weapon sounds were a brief flurry, stilled as quickly as they began. A howl of wounded fury rose and fell, pulsing with the victim's each breath. The sobbing anger guided Cormac and the Vikings behind him along a track no higher than the shoulders of the red deer who wore it. Cormac ran hunched over, accepting the risk of surprise against the desperate need for haste. Two Picts, dead or numb with death's approach, lay along the trail.

The ground sloped up from the creek. Rolf and his captive had burst through the first rush of their attackers and run upward, instinctively seeking high ground. A hundred yards beyond the creek the fugitives had found shelter of a sort.

Weathering between the sedimentary layers of a limestone escarpment had gouged a broad notch six feet above present ground level. In that cavity a blood-stained, blond-haired Viking now glowered down at thirty or more Picts. The tribe's leader—priest or chieftain, Cormac knew not—waved a baton topped with a skull into which was set a pattern of colored pebbles.

The notch was no cave. The front edge was high enough for the Viking to stand upright, but the upper surface sloped down sharply to join the floor no more than six feet into the cliff. A young woman with Gerinth's features crouched there, holding a Norse dagger. Her right arm was red to the elbow with blood.

Several bodies lay at the foot of escarpment, their state depending on how squarely the great Norse sword had caught them in its stroke. Blood and brains splashed the limestone. Rolf, for it must be he, had his father's broad shoulders and the strength of enraged youth.

Rolf wore his mail shirt, but he'd abandoned his shield in the yawl when the Picts suddenly attacked. The notch was broader than it was deep, so it provided no flank protection. A dozen Picts carried short, crooked bows. While their surviving fellows hung back from the deadly broadsword, the archers sent another flight of arrows at the Viking.

The tiny flint points could not pierce the iron mail, but Rolf's unprotected legs and forearms already dripped blood. A broken arrow dangled from his right cheek, wobbling as he moved. To draw out the barbed head in the haste of battle would have done more damage than to leave it, so Rolf had only snapped the shaft short between two fingers and a thumb.

The Picts had failed to overwhelm their opponent with a head-on assault. Now they thought to bleed him dry with a myriad of small wounds—and they would surely succeed, nothing else appearing.

All this Cormac saw in the instant he tore through the screening alders twenty feet from the battle. The original foes, Viking and Picts, remained too focused on one another to note the arrival of a third force. Rolf bellowed a prayer to Othinn the Sword-God and leaped from the ledge, closing with his enemies.

A Pictish spearman lunged forward and died in a spray of blood. His sectioned legs and torso mingled with those of the archer killed by the same horizontal stroke. A dozen skin-clad warriors converged like bees swarming over a hive-robbing bear. A Pict stabbed Rolf deeply from behind.

Cormac throat-thrust a Pict who goggled in shocked surprise, but the Gael left for the reivers following him the mass who'd brought down Rolf. Cormac's thought was for Helen and the three Picts climbing to the ledge now that the young Viking's armored form no longer guarded it.

The Gael struck to the right, splitting a spine between the shoulder blades. His backstroke nigh decapitated a Pict whose pectoral of tortoiseshell and erne feathers flapped as he tumbled backward from the notch. The third Pict turned cat-quick on the ledge and drove his iron-pointed spear at Cormac's face.

The thrust wavered, nicking only the tip of the Gael's left ear. The Pict pitched forward, dead before Cormac's sword drove through his tattooed chest. The Viking dagger projecting from the Pict's back was stuck deep in the rib bones. Helen almost overbalanced from the ledge with her determination not to lose the weapon.

Cormac cleared his sword and glanced behind him. The battle had finished as quickly as the leading Danes arrived. All the Picts were dead or fled. Unprepared and without armor, they'd had no chance to resist the reivers.

Wulfhere glowered furiously at leafmold splotched with body parts. No blood darkened the bright steel of his axe head. Because he'd been at the steering oar, Wulfhere was the last man out of the *Raven.* The killing was ended before the Danish chief reached the scene of others' carnage.

"Come down, now, lass," Cormac said to the princess. He held out his left hand to aid her. "We're in the service of your brother. We'll take you directly to him and collect the gold he offered for your rescue."

Helen hesitated without speaking. Then, placing her own blood-eyed hand in the Gael's, she jumped easily to the ground.

"Helen!" called Marcus. He carried the Pict leader's baton. He'd sheared in half the skull that surmounted it with the same stroke that killed the man himself. "My love, are you wounded?"

Ignoring her betrothed, the princess stepped to where two of the Danes tossed Pictish bodies from

Rolf's great recumbent form. "Say, the Northman's alive," one of the reivers said.

"Easy enough to change that," said Wulfhere, raising his axe.

"No!" Helen cried, the first words Cormac had heard her speak. She threw herself onto Rolf's bloody mail and turned to face her rescuers with an expression of desperate fury.

"Rolf it was who rescued me!" she said. "He knew what his uncle would do when he learned who I really was. *Rolf* was carrying me to my brother, not for gold but for love's sake. When the Picts offered him his life if he turned me over to sacrifice to their moon god, he made them the answer you see splashed on the rocks around you!"

"She doesn't know what she's saying!" Marcus said. "The ordeal has scattered her wits."

"Princess," said Donal, holding the drawn sword which, now that the fighting was over, looked slightly ridiculous in his hand, "Rolf knew the Picts wouldn't spare him even if he granted their request. He fought for himself, not you."

"What did they swear their oath by, girl?" Wulfhere asked. The Dane hadn't slung his axe again in the double loops on his belt. "Was it by their mother's graves? That's a favorite with Picts, I know."

"Their priest swore by Golka the Moon," Helen said. "He swore that the moon might draw the blood from his veins if he failed to set Rolf free and unharmed on the boat."

Wulfhere looked at Cormac and raised an eyebrow.

The Gael nodded. "That was an oath a Pict would keep," he said. "Rolf knew that as surely as we do. Get up, princess. The boy's young and tough. There are no wounds so deep that he won't recover if we bind them before all his life runs out."

Haltingly, then with a graceful twist that brought

her upright, Helen rose from the form her body had shielded.

"I'm to let a brave man, my blood enemy, live?" Wulfhere said. "Is that it, Gael?"

"Aye," said Cormac, meeting the Dane's gaze squarely.

Wulfhere chuckled. "Well, I never thought to die in bed, did I?" he said. "Bjorn, you know as much of leechcraft as any of us. Do what you can for the lad."

"What happens to the Viking then?" Marcus demanded tensely. His hot brown eyes flicked among the men he'd accompanied, but they passed over Helen's pale face as if she were on a distant island. "Do we leave him here with his boat?"

"Rolf returns with us," Helen said.

Wulfhere chuckled again. The girl flushed and looked at the ground, but she continued, "That was what we planned. I will wed Rolf with my brother's blessing, or I'll share whatever other fate Gerinth offers him."

"Well," Cormac said, "we're paid to return you. What happens then is no affair of ours. I—"

"Princess, are you mad?" Marcus shouted. "Apart from your pledge to me—"

"My brother's pledge to you!" Helen said. "Rolf and I pledged in blood. He's loved me since we met two years ago!"

"Aye, two years ago, after his father raped and looted his way through our land," Marcus said. "Will you send your own sons south to finish the job their grandfather began, princess?"

"The time of blood must end somehow, some day," Helen replied. She flushed again, but now with anger rather than embarrassment. "If I can speed that day by wedding a man who loves me and who risked his life to save mine—so be it, Marcus. So be it!"

Marcus had not sheathed the sword on which dried the blood of the Pictish leader. He lunged forward, swinging his blade not toward Rolf but at the woman he had risked his life to save. Donal tried to grab his fellow Briton but managed only to tangle Cormac's arm as the Gael reached out.

Wulfhere's axe split Marcus' skull with the sound of a melon dropped from a great height.

The Briton's sword dropped. His body went limp. He could not fall until the Dane freed his axe with a quick jerk.

Helen stared in dazed horror.

"There's a hundred pounds of gold riding on your pretty face, girl," Wulfhere said casually. He lifted the hem of Marcus' cloak to wipe his blade. "I couldn't have somebody putting a sword through it, could I?"

Cormac looked down at the corpse in Roman trappings. "His time was past," the Gael said. "Perhaps he saw that too. But we'll carry his body to his people and tell them he died a hero, surrounded by slaughtered Picts."

Helen knelt and began to cry. Her hand gripped Rolf's gashed biceps rather than the body of her former betrothed. Donal stared grimly, then sheathed his sword at last.

"Ho!" called Cormac to the Danish reivers. "Let's get back to the ship and away from here, brothers, before Thorlief makes the same calculations we did!"

SWORDS OF THE NORTHERN SEA

SWORDS OF THE NORTHERN SEA

"Skoal!" The smoke-stained rafters shook as the deep-throated roar went up. Drinking horns clashed and sword hilts beat upon the oaken board. Dirks hacked at the great joints of meat, and under the feet of the revelers gaunt, shaggy wolf-hounds fought over the remnants.

At the head of the board sat Rognor the Red, scourge of the Narrow Seas. The huge Viking meditatively stroked his crimson beard, while his great, arrogant eyes roved about the hall, taking in the familiar scene. A hundred warriors feasted here, waited on by bold-eyed, yellow-haired women and by trembling slaves. Spoils of the Southland were flung about in careless profusion. Rare tapestries and brocades, bales of silk and spice, tables and benches of fine mahogany, curiously chased weapons and delicate masterpieces of art vied with the spoils of the hunt—horns and heads of forest beasts. Thus the Viking proclaimed his mastery over man and beast.

The Northern nations were drunken with victory and conquest. Rome had fallen; Frank, Goth, Vandal and Saxon had looted the fairest possessions of the world. And now these races found themselves hard put to hold their prizes from the wilder, fiercer peoples

125

who swept down on them from the blue mists of the North. The Franks, already settled in Gaul and beginning to show signs of Latinization, found the long, lean galleys of the Norsemen bringing the sword up their rivers; the Goth further south felt the weight of their kinsmen's fury and the Saxons, forcing the Britons westward, found themselves assailed by a more furious foe from the rear. East, west and south to the ends of the world ranged the dragon-beaked long ships of the Vikings.

The Norse had already begun to settle in the Hebrides and the Orkneys, though as yet it was more a rendezvous of pirates than the later colonization. And the lair of Rognor the Red was this isle, called by the Scots Ladbhan, the Picts Golmara and the Norse Valgaard. His word was law, the only law this wild horde recognized; his hand was heavy, his soul ruthless, his range the open world.

The sea-king's eyes ranged about the board, while he nodded slightly in satisfaction. No pirate that sailed the seas could boast a fiercer assortment of fighting men than he; a mixed horde they were, Norsemen and Jutes—big, yellow-bearded men with wild, light eyes. Even now as they feasted they were fully armed and girt in mail, though they had laid aside their horned helmets. A ferocious, wayward race they were, with a latent madness burning in their brains, ready to leap into terrible flame at an instant.

Rognor's gaze turned from them, with their great bare arms heavy with golden armlets, to rest on one who seemed strangely different from the rest. This was a tall, rangily built man, deep-chested and strong, whose square-cut black hair and dark, smooth face contrasted with the yellow manes and beards about him. This man's eyes were narrow slits and of a cold-steel grey, and they, with a number of scars that marred his face, lent him a peculiarly sinister aspect. He wore no gold ornaments of any kind and his mail was of chain mesh instead of the scale type worn by the men about him.

Rognor frowned abstractedly as he eyed this man, but just as he was about to speak, another man entered the huge hall and approached the head of the board. This newcomer was a tall, splendidly made young Viking, beardless but wearing a yellow mustache. Rognor greeted him.

"Hail, Hakon! I have not seen you since yesterday."

"I was hunting wolves in the hills," answered the young Viking, glancing curiously at the dark stranger. Rognor followed his gaze.

"That is one Cormac Mac Art, chief of a band of reivers. His galley was wrecked in the gale last night and he alone won through the breakers to shore. He came to the skalli doors early in the dawn, dripping wet, and argued the carles into bringing him in to me instead of slaying him as they had intended. He offered to prove his right to follow me on the Viking path, and fought my best swordsmen, one after the other, weary as he was. Rane, Tostig and Halfgar he played with as they were children and disarmed each without giving scathe or taking a wound himself."

Hakon turned to the stranger and spoke a courtly greeting, and the Gael answered in kind, with a stately inclination of his head.

"You speak our language well," said the young Viking.

"I have many friends among your people," answered Cormac. Hakon's eyes rested on him strangely for a moment, but the inscrutable eyes of the Gael gave back the gaze, with no hint of what was going on in his mind.

Hakon turned back to the sea-king. Irish pirates were common enough in the Narrow Seas, and their forays carried them sometimes as far as Spain and Egypt, though their ships were far less seaworthy than the long ships of the Vikings. But there was little friendship between the races. When a reiver met a Viking, generally a ferocious battle ensued. They were rivals of the Western seas.

"You have come at a good time, Cormac," Rognor was rumbling. "You will see me take a wife tomorrow. By the hammer of Thor! I have taken many women in my time—from the people of Rome and Spain and Egypt, from the Franks, from the Saxons, and from the Danes, the curse of Loki on them! But never have I married one before. Always I tired of them and gave them to my men for sport. But it is time I thought of sons and so I have found a woman, worthy even of the favors of Rognor the Red. Ho—Osric, Eadwig, bring in the British wench! You shall judge for yourself, Cormac."

Cormac's eyes roved to where Hakon sat. To the casual watcher the young Viking seemed disinterested, almost bored. But the Gael's stare centered on the angle of his firm jaw as he caught the sudden, slight ripple of muscle that betrays controlled tenseness. The Gael's cold eyes flickered momentarily.

Three women entered the feasting-hall, closely followed by the two carles Rognor had sent for them. Two of the women led the third before Rognor, then fell back, leaving her facing him alone.

"See, Cormac," rumbled the Viking: "is she not fit to bear the sons of a king?"

Cormac's eyes traveled impersonally up and down the girl who stood panting with anger before him. A fine, robust figure of young womanhood she was, quite evidently not yet twenty years old. Her proud bosom heaved with angry defiance, and her bearing was that of a young queen rather than a captive. She was clad in the rather scanty finery of a Norse woman, but she was quite apparently not of their race. With her blond hair aud blazing blue eyes, coupled with her snowy skin, she was evidently a Celt; but Cormac knew that she was not one of the softened and

Latinized people of southern Britain. Her carriage and manner were as free and barbaric as that of her captors.

"She is the daughter of a chief of the western Britons," said Rognor; "one of a tribe that never bowed the neck to Rome and now, hemmed between the Saxons on one side and the Picts of the other, holds both at bay. A fighting race! I took her from a Saxon galley, whose chief had in turn taken her captive during an inland raid. The moment I laid eyes on her, I knew she was the girl who should bear my sons. I have held her now for some months, having her taught our ways and language. She was a wildcat when we first caught her! I gave her in charge of old Eadna, a very she-bear of a woman—and by the hammer of Thor, the old valkyrie nearly met her match! It took a dozen birchings across old Eadna's knee to tame the spit-fire—"

"Are you done with me, pirate?" flamed the girl suddenly, defiantly, yet with a tearful catch, barely discernible, in her voice. "If so, let me go back to my chamber—for the hag-face of Eadna, ugly as it is, is more pleasant to my sight than your red-bearded swine-face!"

A roar of mirth went up, and Cormac grinned thinly.

"It seems that her spirit is not utterly broken," he commented dryly.

"I would not count her worth a broken twig if it were," answered the sea-king, unabashed. "A woman without mettle is like a scabbard without a sword. You may return to your chamber, my pretty one, and prepare for your nuptials on the morrow. Mayhap you will look on me with more favor after you have borne me three or four stout sons!"

The girl's eyes snapped blue fire, but without a word she turned her back squarely on her master and prepared to leave the hall—when a voice suddenly cut through the din:

"*Hold!*"

Cormac's eyes narrowed as a grotesque and abhorrent figure came shambling and lurching across the hall. It was a creature with the face of a mature man, but it was no taller than a young boy, and its body was strangely deformed with twisted legs, huge malformed feet and one shoulder much higher than the other. Yet the fellow's breadth and girth were surprising; a stunted, malformed giant he seemed. From a dark, evil face gleamed two great, yellow eyes.

"What is this?" asked the Gael. "I knew you Vikings sailed far, but I never heard that you sailed to the gates of Hell. Yet surely this thing had its birth nowhere else."

Rognor grinned. "Aye, in Hell I caught him, for in many ways Byzantium is Hell, where the Greeks break and twist the bodies of babes that they may grow into such blasphemies as this, to furnish sport for the emperor and his nobles. What now Anzace?"

"Great lord," wheezed the creature in a shrill, loathly voice, "tomorrow you take this girl, Tarala, to wife—is it not? Aye—oh, aye! But, mighty lord, what if she loves another?"

Tarala had turned back and now bent on the dwarf a wide-eyed stare in which aversion and anger vied with fear.

"Love another?" Rognor drank deep and wiped his beard. "What of it? Few girls love the men they have to marry. What care I for her love?"

"Ah," sneered the dwarf, "but would you care if I told you that one of your own men talked to her last night—aye, and for many nights before that—through the bars of her window?"

Down crashed the drinking-jack. Silence fell over the hall and all eyes turned toward the group at the head of the table. Hakon rose, flushing angrily.

"Rognor—" his hand trembled on his sword—"if you will allow this vile creature to insult your wife-to-be, I at least—"

"He lies!" cried the girl, reddening with shame and rage. "I—"

"Be silent!" roared Rognor. "You, too, Hakon. As for you—" his huge hand shot out and closed like a vise on the front of Anzace's tunic—"speak, and speak quickly. If you lie—you die!"

The dwarf's dusky hue paled slightly, but he shot a spiteful glance of reptilian malice toward Hakon. "My lord," said he, "I have watched for many a night since I first saw the glances this girl exchanged with he who has betrayed you. Last night, lying close among the trees without her window, I heard them plan to flee tonight. You are to be robbed of your fine bride, master."

Rognor shook the Greek as a mastiff shakes a rat. "Dog!" he roared. "Prove this or howl under the blood-eagle!"

"I can prove it," purred the dwarf. "Last night I had another with me—one who you know is a speaker of truth. Tostig!"

A tall, cruel-visaged warrior came forward, his manner one of sullen defiance. He was one of those on whom Cormac had proved his swordsmanship.

"Tostig," grinned the dwarf, "tell our master whether I speak truth—tell him if you lay in the bushes with me last night and heard his most trusted man—who was supposed to be up in the hills hunting—plot with this yellow-haired wench to betray their master and flee tonight."

"He speaks truth," said the Norseman sullenly.

"Odin, Thor and Loki!" snarled Rognor, flinging the dwarf from him and crashing his fist down on the board. "And who was the traitor?—tell me, that I may break his vile neck with my two hands!"

"*Hakon!*" screamed the dwarf, a quivering finger

stabbing at the young Viking, his face writhing in a horrid contortion of venomous triumph. "Hakon, your right hand man!"

"Aye, Hakon it was," growled Tostig.

Rognor's jaw dropped, and for an instant a tense silence gripped the hall. Then Hakon's sword was out like a flash of summer lightning and he sprang like a wounded panther at his betrayers. Anzace screeched and turned to run, and Tostig drew back and parried Hakon's whistling stroke. But the fury of that headlong attack was not to be denied. Hakon's single terrific blow shivered Tostig's sword and flung the warrior at Rognor's feet, brains oozing from his cleft skull. At the same time Tarala, with the desperate fury of a tigress, snatched up a bench and dealt Anzace such a blow as to stretch him stunned and bleeding on the floor.

The whole hall was in an uproar. Warriors roared their bewilderment and indecision as they shouldered each other and snarled out of the corners of their mouths, gripping their weapons and quivering with eagerness for action, but undecided which course to follow. Their two leaders were at variance, and their loyalty wavered. But close about Rognor were a group of hardened veterans who were assailed by no doubts. Their duty was to protect their chief at all times and this they now did, moving in a solid hedge against the enraged Hakon who was making a most sincere effort to detach the head of his former ally from its shoulders. Left alone, the matter might have been in doubt, but Rognor's vassals had no intention of leaving their chief to fight his own battles. They closed in on Hakon, beat down his guard by the very weight of their numbers and stretched him on the floor, bleeding from a dozen minor cuts, where he was soon bound hand and foot. All up and down the hall the rest of the horde was pressing forward, exclaiming and swearing at each other, and there was some muttering and some black glances cast at Rognor; but the sea-king, sheathing the great sword with which he had been parrying Hakon's vicious cuts, pounded on the board and shouted ferociously. The insurgents sank back, muttering, quelled by the blast of his terrific personality.

Anzace rose, glassy-eyed and holding his head. A great, bleak woman had wrested the bench away from Tarala and now held the blond girl tucked under her arm like an infant, while Tarala kicked and struggled and cursed. In the whole hall there was but one person who seemed not to share the general frenzy—the Gaelic pirate, who had not risen from his seat where he sipped his ale with a cynical smile.

"You would betray me, eh?" bellowed Rognor, kicking his former lieutenant viciously. "You whom I trusted, whom I raised to high honor—" Words failed the outraged sea-king and he brought his feet into play again, while Tarala shrieked wrathful protests:

"Beast! Thief! Coward! If he were free you would not dare!"

"Be silent!" roared Rognor.

"I will not be silent!" she raged, kicking vainly in the old woman's grasp. "I love him! Why should I not love him in preference to you? Where you are harsh and cruel, he is kind. He is brave and courteous, and the only man among you that has treated me with consideration in my captivity. I will marry him or no other—"

With a roar Rognor drew back his iron fist, but before he could crash it into that defiant, beautiful face, Cormac rose and caught his wrist. Rognor grunted involuntarily; the Gael's fingers were like steel. For a moment the Norseman's flaming eyes glared into the cold eyes of Cormac and neither wavered.

"You cannot marry a dead woman, Rognor," said

Cormac coolly. He released the other's wrist and resumed his seat.

The sea-king growled something in his beard and shouted to his grim vassals: "Take this young dog and chain him in the cell; tomorrow he shall watch me marry the wench, and then *she* shall watch while with my own hands I cut the blood-eagle in his back."

Two huge carles stolidly lifted the bound and raging Hakon, and as they started to bear him from the hall, he fell suddenly silent and his gaze rested full on the sardonic face of Cormac Mac Art. The Gael returned the glance, and suddenly Hakon spat a single word: "Wolf!"

Cormac did not start; not by the flicker of an eye-lash did he betray any surprise. His inscrutable gaze did not alter as Hakon was borne from the hall.

"What of the wench, master?" asked the woman who held Tarala captive. "Shall I not strip her and birch her?"

"Prepare her for the marrying," growled Rognor with an impatient gesture. "Take her out of my sight before I lose my temper and break her white neck!"

A torch in a niche of the wall flickered, casting an indistinct light about the small cell, whose floor was of dirt and whose walls and roof were of square-cut logs. Hakon the Viking, chained in the corner furthest from the door, just beneath the small, heavily-barred window, shifted his position and cursed fervently. It was neither his chains nor his wounds which caused his discomfiture. The wounds were slight and had already begun to heal—and, besides, the Norsemen were inured to unbelievable physical discomforts. Nor was the thought of death what made him writhe and curse. It was the reflection that Rognor was going to take Tarala for his unwilling bride and that he, Hakon, was unable to prevent it ...

He froze as a light, wary step sounded outside.

Then he heard a voice say, with an alien accent: "Rognor desires me to talk with the prisoner."

"How do I know you speak truth?" grumbled the guard.

"Go and ask Rognor; I will stand guard while you go. If he flays your back for disturbing him, don't blame me."

"Go in, in the name of Loki," snarled the guard. "But do not tarry too long."

There was a fumbling of bolts and bars; the door swung open, framing a tall, lithe form; then it closed again. Cormac Mac Art looked down at the prostrate Hakon. Cormac was fully armed, and on his head he wore a helmet with a crest ornamented with flowing horse hair. This seemed to make him inhumanly tall and, in the flickering, illusive light which heightened the darkness and sinisterness of his appearance, the Gaelic pirate seemed not unlike some sombre demon come to taunt a captive in a shadowy corner of Hell.

"I thought you would come," said Hakon, rising to a sitting position. "Speak softly, however, lest the guard outside hear us."

"I came because I wished to know where you learned my language," said the Gael.

"You lie," replied Hakon cheerfully. "You came lest I betray you to Rognor. When I spoke the name men have given you, in your own tongue, you knew that I knew who you really were. For that name means 'Wolf' in your language, and you are not only Cormac Mac Art of Erin, but you are Cormac the Wolf, a reiver and a killer, and the right-hand man of Wulfhere the Dane, Rognor's greatest enemy. What you are doing here I know not, but I do know that the presence of Wulfhere's closest comrade means no good for Rognor. I have but to say a word to the guard and your fate is as certain as mine."

Cormac looked down at the youth and was silent for a moment.

"I might cut your throat before you could speak," he said.

"You might," agreed Hakon, "but you won't. It is not in you to slay a defenseless man thus."

Cormac grinned bleakly. "True. What would you have of me?"

"My life for yours. Get me free and I keep your secret till Ragnarok."

Cormac seated himself on a small stool and meditated.

"What are your plans?"

"Free me—and let me get my hands on a sword. I'll steal Tarala and we will seek to gain the hills. If not, I'll take Rognor with me to Valhalla."

"And if you gain the hills?"

"I have men waiting there—fifteen of my closest friends, Jutes, mainly, who have no love for Rognor. On the other side of the island we have hidden a longboat. In it we can win to another island where we can hide from Rognor until we have a band of our own. Masterless men and runaway carles will come to us and it may not be long until I can burn Rognor's skalli over his head and pay him back for his kicks."

Cormac nodded. In that day of pirates and raiders, outlaws and reivers, such a thing as Hakon suggested was common enough.

"But first you must escape from this cell."

"That is your part," rejoined the youth.

"Wait," said the Gael. "You say you have fifteen friends in the forest—"

"Aye—on pretext of a wolf hunt we went up into the hills yesterday and I left them at a certain spot, while I slipped back and made the rest of my plans with Tarala. I was to spend the day at the skalli, and then, pretending to go for my friends tonight, I was to ride forth, returning stealthily and stealing Tarala. I reckoned not on Anzace, that Byzantium he-witch, whose foul heart, I swear, I will give to the kites—"

"Enough," snapped Cormac impatiently. "Have you any friends among the carles now in the steading? Methought I noted some displeasure among them at your rough handling."

"I have a number of friends and half-friends," answered Hakon, "but they waver—a carle is a stupid animal and apt to follow whoever seems strongest. Let Rognor fall, with his band of chosen henchmen, and the rest would likely as not join my forces."

"Good enough." Cormac's eyes glittered as his keen brain began racing with an idea. "Now, listen—I told Rognor truth when I said my galley was dashed on the rocks last night—but I lied when I said only I escaped. Well hidden beyond the southern point of this island, where the sand spits run out into the surf, is Wulfhere with fifty-odd swordsmen. When we fought through the madness of the breakers last night and found ourselves ashore with no ship and only a part of our band left alive—and on Rognor's island— we took council and decided that I, whom Rognor was less likely to know, should go boldly up to his skalli and, getting into his favor, look for a chance to outwit him and seize one of his galleys. For it is a ship we want. Now I will bargain with you. If I help you to escape, will you join your forces with mine and Wulfhere's and aid us to overthrow Rognor? And, having overthrown him, will you give us one of his long ships? That is all we ask. The loot of the skalli and all Rognor's carles and the rest of his ships shall be all yours. With a good long ship under our feet, Wulfhere and I will soon gain plunder enough—aye, and Vikings for a full crew."

"It is a bargain," promised the youth. "Aid me and I aid you; make me lord of this island with your help and you shall have the pick of the long ships."

"Good enough; now attend me. Is your guard likely to be changed tonight?"

"Scarcely, I think."

"Think you he could be bribed, Hakon?"

"Not he. He is one of Rognor's picked band."

"Well, then we must try some other way. If we can dispose of him, your escape will hardly be discovered before morning. Wait!"

The Gael stepped to the door of the cell and spoke to the guard.

"What sort of a watchman are you, to leave a way of escape for your prisoner?"

"What mean you?" The Viking's beard bristled.

"Why, all the bars have been torn from the window."

"You are mad!" growled the warrior, entering the cell. He raised his head to stare at the window, and even as his chin rose at an angle following his eyes, Cormac's iron fist, backed by every ounce of his mighty body, crashed against the Viking's jaw. The fellow dropped like a slaughtered ox, senseless.

The key to Hakon's chains was at the guard's girdle. In an instant the young Viking rose, free of his bonds, and Cormac, having gagged the unconscious warrior and chained him in turn, handed it to Hakon who grasped it eagerly. No word was said as the two stole from the cell and into the shadows of the surrounding trees. There Cormac halted. He eyed the steading keenly. There was no moon but the starlight was sufficient for the Gael's purposes.

The skalli, a long rambling structure of logs, faced the bay where Rognor's galleys rode at anchor. Grouped about the main building in a rough half circle were the store houses, the huts of the carles and the stables. A hundred or so yards separated the nearest of these from the skalli, and the hut wherein Hakon had been pent was the furthest away from the hall. The forest pressed closely on three sides, the tall trees overshadowing many of the store houses. There was no wall or moat about Rognor's steading. He was sole lord of the island and expected no raid from the land side. At any rate, his steading was not intended as a fortress but as a sort of camp from which he swooped down on his victims.

While Cormac was taking in all salient points, his quick ears caught a stealthy footstep. Straining his eyes, he glimpsed the hint of a movement under the thick trees. Beckoning Hakon, he crept silently forward, dirk in hand. The brooding shadows masked all, but Cormac's wild beast instinct, that comes to men who live by their wits, told him that someone or something was gliding through the darkness close at hand. A twig snapped faintly some little distance away, and then, a moment later, he saw a vague shape detach itself from the blackness of the trees and drift swiftly toward the skalli. Even in the dimness of the starlight the creature seemed abnormal and uncanny.

"Anzace!" hissed Hakon, electrified. "He was hiding in the trees, watching the cell! Stop him, quickly!"

Cormac's grip on his arm stayed him from springing out recklessly in pursuit.

"Silence!" hissed the Gael. "He knows you are free, but he may not know we know it. We have yet time before he reaches Rognor."

"But Tarala!" exclaimed Hakon fiercely. "I'll not leave her alone here now. Go if you will—I'll steal her away now, or die here!"

Cormac glanced quickly toward the skalli. Anzace had vanished around the corner. Apparently he was making for the front entrance.

"Lead to the girl's chamber," growled Cormac. "It's a desperate chance—but Rognor might cut her throat when he learns we've fled, before we could return and rescue her."

Hakon and his companion, emerging from the shadows, ran swiftly across the open starlit space which parted the forest from the skalli. The young Norseman led the way to a heavily barred window near the rear end of the long, rambling hall. Crouching there in the shadows of the building, he rapped cautiously on the bars, three times. Almost instantly Tarala's white face was framed dimly in the aperture.

"Hakon!" came the passionate whisper. "Oh, be careful! Old Eadna is in the room with me. She is asleep, but—"

"Stand back," whispered Hakon, raising his sword. "I'm going to hew these bars apart—"

"The clash of metal will wake every carle on the island," grunted Cormac. "We have a few minutes leeway while Anzace is telling his tale to Rognor. Let you not throw it away."

"But how else—?"

"Stand away," growled the Gael, gripping a bar in each hand and bracing his feet and knees against the wall. Hakon's eyes widened as he saw Cormac arch his back and throw every ounce of his incredible frame into the effort. The young Viking saw the great muscles writhe and ripple along the Gael's arms, shoulders and legs; the veins stood out on Cormac's temples, and then, before the astounded eyes of the watchers the bars bent and gave way, literally torn from their sockets. A dull, rending crash resulted, and in the room someone stirred with a startled exclamation.

"Quick, through the window!" snapped Cormac fiercely, galvanized back into dynamic action in spite of the terrific strain of his feat.

Tarala flung one limb over the shattered sill—then there sounded a low, fierce exclamation behind her and a quick rush. A pair of thick, clutching hands closed on the girl's shoulders—and then, twisting about, Tarala struck a heavy blow. The hands went limp and there was the sound of a falling body. In another instant the British girl was out of the window and in the arms of her lover.

"There!" she gasped breathlessly, half sobbing, throwing aside the heavy wine goblet with which she had knocked her guard senseless. "That pays old Eadna back for some of the spankings she gave me!"

"Haste!" rapped Cormac, urging the pair toward the forest. "The whole steading will be roused in a moment—"

Already lights were flaring and Rognor's bull voice was heard bellowing. In the shadows of the trees Cormac halted an instant.

"How long will it take you to reach your men in the hills and return here?"

"Return here?"

"Yes."

"Why—an hour and a half at the utmost."

"Good!" snapped the Gael. "Conceal your men on yonder side of the clearing and wait until you hear this signal—" And he cautiously made the sound of a night bird thrice repeated.

"Come to me—alone—when you hear that sound—and take care to avoid Rognor and his men as you come—"

"Why—he'll most certainly wait until morning before he begins searching the island."

Cormac laughed shortly. "Not if I know him. He'll be out with all his men combing the woods tonight. But we've wasted too much time—see, the steading is aswarm with armed warriors. Get your Jutes back here as soon as you may. I'm for Wulfhere."

Cormac waited until the girl and her lover had vanished in the shadows, then he turned and ran fleetly and silently as the beast for which he was named. Where the average man would have floundered and blundered through the shadows, caroming into trees and tripping over bushes, Cormac sped lightly and easily, guided partly by his eyes, mainly by his unerring instinct. A lifetime in the forests and on the seas of the wild northern and eastern countries had given him the thews, wits and endurance of the fierce beasts that roamed there.

Behind him he heard shouts, clashing of arms and a bloodthirsty voice roaring threats and blasphemies. Evidently Rognor had discovered that both his birds had flown. These sounds grew fainter as he rapidly increased the distance between, and presently the Gael heard the low lapping of waves against the sand bars. As he approached the hiding-place of his allies, he slackened his pace and went more cautiously. His Danish friends lacked somewhat of his ability to see in the dark, and the Gael had no wish to stop an arrow intended for an enemy.

He halted and sounded the low pitched call of the wolf. Almost instantly came an answer, and he went forward with more assurance. Soon a vague huge figure rose in the shadows in front of him and a rough voice accosted him.

"Cormac—by Thor, we had about decided you failed to trick them—"

"They are slow witted fools," answered the Gael. "But I know not if my plan shall succeed. We are only some seventy to over three hundred."

"Seventy—why—?"

"We have some allies now—you know Hakon, Rognor's mate?"

"Aye."

"He has turned against his chief and now moves against him with fifteen Jutes—or will shortly. Come, Wulfhere, order out the warriors. We go to throw the dice of chance again. If we lose, we gain an honorable death; if we win, we gain a goodly long ship, and you—vengeance!"

"Vengeance!" murmured Wulfhere softly. His fierce eyes gleamed in the starlight and his huge hand locked like iron about the handle of his battle-axe. A red-bearded giant was the Dane, as tall as Cormac and more heavily built. He lacked something of the Gael's tigerish litheness but he made up for that in oak-and-iron massiveness. His horned helmet increased the barbaric wildness of his appearance.

"Out of your dens, wolves!" he called into the darkness behind him. "Out! No more skulking for Wulfhere's killers—we go to feed the ravens. Osric—Halfgar—Edric—Athelgard—Aslaf—out, wolves, the feast is ready!"

As if born from the night and the shadows of the brooding trees, the warriors silently took shape. There were few words spoken and the only sounds were the occasional rattle of a belt chain or the rasp of a swinging scabbard. Single file they trailed out behind their leaders, and Cormac, glancing back, saw only a sinuous line of great, vague forms, darker shadows amid the shadows, with a swaying of horns above. To his imaginative Celtic mind it seemed that he led a band of horned demons through the midnight forest.

At the crest of a small rise, Cormac halted so suddenly that Wulfhere, close behind, bumped into him. The Gael's steel fingers closed on the Viking's arm, halting his grumbled question. Ahead of them came a sudden murmur and a rattle of weapons, and now lights shone through the trees.

"Lie down!" hissed Cormac, and Wulfhere obeyed, growling the order back to the men behind. As one man, they prostrated themselves and lay silently. The noise grew louder swiftly, the tramp of many men. Presently into view came a motley horde of men, waving torches as they scanned all sides of the sullen forest, whose menacing darkness the torches but accentuated. They were following a dim trail which cut across Cormac's line of march. In front of them strode Rognor, his face black with passion, his eyes terrible. He gnawed his beard as he strode, and his great sword trembled in his hand. Close behind him came his picked swordsmen in a compact, immobile-faced clump, and behind them the rest of the carles strung out in a straggling horde.

At the sight of his enemy Wulfhere shivered as with a chill. Under Cormac's restraining hand the great thews of his arm swelled and knotted into ridges of iron.

"A flight of arrows, Cormac," he urged in a passionate whisper, his voice heavy with hate. "Let's loose a rain of shafts into them and then lash in with the blades—"

"No, not now!" hissed the Gael. "There are nearly three hundred men with Rognor. He is playing into our hands and we must not lose the chance the gods have given us! Lie still and let them pass!"

Not a sound betrayed the presence of the fifty-odd Danes as they lay like the shadow of Doom above the slope. The Norsemen passed at right angles and vanished in the forest beyond without having seen or heard anything of the men whose fierce eyes watched them. Cormac nodded grimly. He had been right when he assumed that Rognor would not wait for the dawn before combing the island for his captive and her abductor. Here in this forest, where fifty-odd men could escape the eyes of the searchers, Rognor could scarcely have hoped to find the fugitives. But the fury that burned in the Norseman's brain would not allow him to keep still while those who defied him were still at liberty. It was not in a Viking to sit still when fired with rage, even though action were useless. Cormac knew these strange, fierce people better than they knew themselves.

Not until the clash of steel had died out in the forest beyond, and the torchlights had become mere fire-flies glimpsed occasionally through the trees, did Cormac give the order to advance. Then at double quick time they hastened on, until they saw more lights ahead of them, and presently, crouching beneath the tall trees at the edge of the clearing, looked out on the steading of Rognor the Red. The main skalli and many of the smaller buildings were alight but only a few warriors were seen. Evidently Rognor had taken most of his carles with him on his useless chase.

"What now, Cormac?" said Wulfhere.

"Hakon should be here," answered Cormac. Even as he opened his mouth to give the signal agreed upon, a carle rounded the corner of a stable close by, carrying a torch. The watchers saw him alter his leisurely pace suddenly and glance fixedly in their direction. Some motion in the deep shadows had attracted his attention.

"What cursed luck!" hissed Wulfhere. "He's coming straight for us. Edric—lose me an arrow—"

"No," muttered Cormac, "never kill, Wulfhere, save when it is necessary. Wait!"

The Gael faded back into the darkness like a phantom. The carle came straight for the forest edge, waving his torch slightly, curious, but evidently not suspicious. Now he was under the trees and his outthrust fagot shone full on Wulfhere, where the huge Dane stood in grim silence, motionless as a statue.

"Rognor!" The flickering light was illusive; the carle saw only a red-bearded giant. "Back so soon? Have you caught—?"

The sentence broke off abruptly as he saw the red beards and fierce, unfamiliar faces of the silent men ranged behind Wulfhere; his gaze switched back to the chief and his eyes flared with sudden horror. His lips parted, but at that instant an iron arm hooked about his throat, strangling the threatened yell. Wulfhere knocked the torch from his hand and stamped it out, and in the darkness the carle was disarmed and bound securely with his own harness.

"Speak low and answer my questions," sounded a sinister whisper at his ear. "How many weapon-men are there left at the steading?"

The carle was brave enough in open battle, but the suddenness of the surprise had unnerved him, and here in the darkness, surrounded by his ruthless hereditary foes, with the demonic Gael muttering at his shoulder, the Norseman's blood turned to ice.

"Thirty men remain," he answered.

"Where are they?"

"Half of them are in the skalli. The rest are in the huts."

"Good enough," grunted the Gael. "Gag him and bring him along with us. Now wait here until I find Hakon."

He gave the cry of a sleepy bird, thrice repeated, and waited a moment. The answer came drifting back from the woods on the other side of the clearing.

"Stay here," ordered the Gael, and melted from the sight of Wulfhere and his Danes like a shadow.

Cautiously he made his way around the fringe of the forest, keeping well hidden in the trees, and presently a slight rustling noise ahead of him made him aware that a body of men lurked before him. He sounded the signal again, and presently heard Hakon whisper a sibilant warning. Behind the young Viking the Gael made out the vague forms of his warriors.

"By the gods," muttered Cormac impatiently, "you make enough noise to wake Caesar. Surely the carles had investigated but that they thought you a herd of buffalo—who is this?"

By Hakon's side was a slim figure, clad in mail and armed with a sword, but strangely out of place among the giant warriors.

"Tarala," answered Hakon. "She would not stay hidden in the hills—so I found a corselet that she could wear and—"

Cormac cursed fervently. "Well—well. Now attend me closely. See you yon hut—the one wherein you were confined? Well, we are going to set fire to it."

"But, man," exclaimed Hakon, "the flame will bring Rognor on the run!"

"Exactly; that is what I wish. Now when the fire brings the carles running, you and your Jutes sally from the forest and fall upon them. Cut down as many as you can, but the moment they rally and make head against you, fall back into the stables, which you can easily do. If you work it right, you should do this without losing a man. Then, once inside the stable, bar and bolt the doors and hold it against them. They will not set fire to it, because many fine horses are there, and you with your men can hold it easily against thirty."

"But what of you and your Danes?" protested Hakon. "Are we to bear all the brunt and danger, while—"

Cormac's hand shot out and his steely fingers sank fiercely in Hakon's shoulder.

"Do you trust me or do you not?" he snarled. "By the blood of the gods, are we to waste the night in argument? Do you not see that so long as Rognor's men think they have only you to deal with, the surprise will be triply effective when Wulfhere strikes? Worry not—when the time comes my Danes will drink blood aplenty."

"Well enough," agreed Hakon, convinced by the dynamic impact of the Gael's will, "but you must have Tarala with you, out of harm's way for the time—"

"Never!" cried the girl, stamping her small foot. "I shall be at your side, Hakon, as long as we both live. I am the daughter of a British prince and I can wield a sword as well as any of your men!"

"Well," Cormac grinned thinly, "easy to see who'll be the real ruler in your family—but come, we have no time to waste. Leave her here with your men for now."

As they glided through the shadows, Cormac repeated his plans in a low voice, and soon they stood at the point where the forest most nearly approached the hut that served as Rognor's prison. Warily they stole from the trees and swiftly ran to the hut. A large tree stood just without the door and as they passed under it, something bumped heavily against Cormac's face. His quick hand grasped a human foot and, looking up in surprise, he made out a vague figure swaying limply to and fro above him.

"Your jailor!" he grunted. "That was ever Rognor's way, Hakon—when in anger, hang the first man handy. A poor custom—never kill except when necessary."

The logs of the hut were dry, with much bark still on them. A few seconds' work with flint and steel and a thin wisp of flame caught the shredded fibre and curled up the wall.

"Back to your men, now," muttered Cormac, "and wait until the carles are swarming about the huts. Then hack straight through them and gain the stables."

Hakon nodded and darted away. A few minutes more found Cormac back with his own men, who were muttering restlessly as they watched the flames eat their way up the wall of the hut. Suddenly a shout sounded from the skalli. Men came pouring out of the main hall and the huts, some fully armed and wide awake, some gaping and half clad as though just awakened from a sound sleep. Behind them peered the women and slaves. The men snatched buckets of water and ran for the hut and in a moment the scene was one of the usual confusion attendant to a fire. The carles jostled each other, shouted useless advice and made a vain attempt to stem the flame which now leaped roaring up through the roof and curled high in a blaze that was sure to be seen by Rognor wherever he was.

And in the midst of the turmoil there sounded a fierce medley of yells and a small, compact body of men crashed from the forest and smote the astonished carles like a thunderbolt. Hacking and hewing right and left, Hakon and his Jutes cleft their way through the bewildered Norsemen, leaving a wake of dead and dying behind them.

Wulfhere trembled with eagerness and behind him his Danes snarled and tensed like hunting dogs straining at the leash.

"How now, Cormac," cried the Viking chief, "shall we not strike a blow? My axe is hungry!"

"Be patient, old sea-wolf," grinned Cormac savagely. "Your axe shall drink deep; see, Hakon and his Jutes have gained the stable and shut the doors."

It was true. The Norsemen had recovered from their surprise and prepared to turn on their attackers with all the fury that characterized their race, but before they could make any headway, Hakon and his men had disappeared inside the stable whence came the neighing and stamping of frightened horses.

This stable, built to withstand the inroads of hunger-maddened wolves and the ravages of a Baltic winter, was a natural fortress, and against its heavy panels the axes of the carles thundered in vain. The only way into the building was through the windows. The heavy wooden bars that guarded these were soon hacked away, but climbing through them in the teeth of the defenders' swords was another. After a few disastrous attempts, the survivors drew off and consulted with each other. As Cormac had reasoned, burning the stable was out of the question because of the blooded horses within. Nor was a flight of arrows through the windows logical. All was dark inside the stable and a chance flown shaft was more likely to hit a horse than a man. Outside, however, the whole steading was lit like day by the burning hut; the Jutes were not famed as archers, but there were a few bows among Hakon's men and these did good execution among the men outside.

At last a carle shouted: "Rognor will have seen the fire and be returning—Olaf, run you and meet him, and tell him Hakon and his Jutes are pent in the stable. We will surround the place and keep them there until Rognor gets here. Then we shall see!"

A carle set off at full speed and Cormac laughed softly to himself.

"Just what I was hoping for! The gods have been good to us this night, Wulfhere! But back—further into the shadows, lest the flames discover us."

Then followed a tense time of waiting for all concerned—for the Jutes imprisoned in the stable, for the Norsemen lying about it, and for the unseen Danes lurking just within the forest edge. The fire burnt itself out and the flames died in smoking embers. Away in the east shone the first touch of dawn. A wind blew up from the sea and stirred the forest leaves. And through the woods echoed the tramp of many men, the clash of steel and deep angry shouts. Cormac's nerves hummed like taut lute strings. Now was the crucial moment. If Rognor's men passed from the forest into the clearing without seeing their hidden foes, all was well. Cormac made the Danes lie prone and, with heart in his mouth, waited.

Again came the glimmer of torches through the trees, and with a sigh of relief Cormac saw that Rognor was approaching the steading from another direction than that he had taken in leaving it. The motley horde broke cover almost opposite the point where Cormac and his men lay.

Rognor was roaring like a wild bull and swinging his two-handed sword in great arcs.

"Break down the doors!" he shouted. "Follow me— shatter the walls!"

The whole horde streamed out across the clearing, Rognor and his veterans in the lead.

Wulfhere had leaped to his feet and his Danes rose

as a man behind him. The chief's eyes were blazing with battle-lust.

"Wait!" Cormac thrust him back. "Wait until they are pounding at the doors!"

Rognor's Vikings crashed headlong against the stable. They bunched at the windows, stabbing and hacking at the blades that thrust from within. The clash of steel rose deafeningly, frightened horses screamed and kicked thunderously at their stalls, while the heavy doors shook to the impact of a hundred axes.

"*Now!*" Cormac leaped to his feet, and across the clearing swept a sudden storm of arrows. Men went down in windrows, and the rest turned bewilderedly to face this sudden and unguessed foe. The Danes were bowmen as well as swordsmen; they excelled all other nations of the North in this art. Now as they leaped from their hiding place, they loosed their shafts as they ran with unerring aim. But the Norsemen were not ready to break yet. Seeing their red-maned foes charging them, they supposed, dazedly, that a great host was upon them, but with the reckless valor of their breed they leaped to meet them.

Driving their last flight of shafts point-blank, the Danes dropped their bows and leaped into close quarters, yelling like fiends, to slash and hack with swords and axes.

They were far outnumbered, but the surprise told heavily and the unexpected arrows had taken terrific toll. Still Cormac, slashing and thrusting with reddened sword, knew that their only chance lay in a quick victory. Let the battle be drawn out and the superior numbers of the Norse must win. Hakon and his Jutes had sallied from the stable and were assailing their former mates from that side. There in the first white light of dawn was enacted a scene of fury.

Rognor, thought Cormac as he mechanically dodged an axe and ran the wielder through, must die quickly if the coup he wished for was to be brought about.

And now he saw Rognor and Wulfhere surging toward each other through the waves of battle. A Dane, thrusting savagely at the Norseman, went down with a shattered skull, and then with a thunderous yell of fury the two red-bearded giants crashed together. All the pent up ferocity of years of hatred burst into flame, and the opposing hordes halted their own fight mutually to watch their chieftains battle.

There was little to choose between them in size and strength. Rognor was armed with a great sword that he swung in both hands, while Wulfhere bore a long-shafted axe and a heavy shield. That shield was rent in twain beneath Rognor's first incredible stroke, and tossing the fragments away, Wulfhere struck back and hewed one of the horns from the Norseman's helmet. Rognor roared and cut terrifically at Wulfhere's legs, but the huge Dane, with a quickness astounding in a man of his bulk, bounded high in the air, cleared the whistling blade and in mid-air chopped down at Rognor's head. The heavy axe struck glancingly on the iron helmet, but even so Rognor went to his knees with a grunt. Then even as the Dane heaved up his axe for another stroke, Rognor was up and his mighty arms brought down his great sword in an arc that crashed full on Wulfhere's helmet. The huge blade shivered with a tremendous crash and Wulfhere staggered, his eyes filling with blood. Like a wounded tiger he struck back with all the might of his gigantic frame, and his blind, terrible stroke cleft Rognor's helmet and shattered the skull beneath. Both hosts cried out at the marvel of that blow as Rognor's corpse tumbled at Wulfhere's feet— and the next instant the blinded giant went down before a perfect storm of swords as Rognor's picked swordsmen rushed to avenge their chief.

With a yell Cormac bounded into the press and his

sword wove a web of death above the chief who, having grappled with some of his attackers, now kicked and wrestled with them on the bloody earth. The Danes surged in to aid their leaders, and about the fallen chieftains eddied a whirlpool of steel. Cormac found himself opposed to Rane, one of Rognor's prize swordsmen, while Hakon battled with his mate, Halfgar. Cormac laughed; he had crossed swords with Rane, a lean shaggy wolf of a man, that morning and he knew all he wished to know about him. A quick parry of an overhand stroke, a dazzling feint to draw a wide lunge, and the Gael's sword was through the Viking's heart.

Then he turned to Hakon. The young Viking was hard pressed; Halfgar, a giant, taller than Wulfhere, towered over him, raining terrific blows upon his shield so swiftly Hakon could make no attempt to launch an offensive of his own. An unusually vicious stroke beat his helmet down over his eyes and for an instant he lost touch of his opponent's blade. In that instant he would have died, but a slim, girlish figure leaped in front of him and took the blow on her own blade, the force of it dashing her to her knees. Up went the giant's sword again—but at that second Cormac's point pierced his bull throat just above the mail.

Then the Gael wheeled back, just as a powerful carle raised an axe high above the still prostrate Wulfhere. The point was Cormac's favorite, but that he could use the edge as well he proved by splitting the carle's skull to the chin. Then, grabbing Wulfhere's shoulders, he hauled him off the men he was seeking to throttle and dragged him, cursing and bellowing like a bull, out of the press.

A quick glance showed him that Rognor's veterans had fallen before the axes of the Danes, and that the rest of the Norsemen, seeing their chief fall, had renewed the fight only halfheartedly. Then what he had hoped for occurred. One of the Norsemen shouted: "The woods are full of Danes!" And the strange, inexplicable panic that sometimes seizes men gripped the carles. Shouting, they gave back and fled for the skalli in a straggling body. Wulfhere, shaking the blood out of his eyes and bellowing for his axe, would have hurled his men after them, but Cormac stopped him. His shouted commands kept the Danes from following the fugitives, who were fortified in the skalli and ready to sell their lives as dearly as only cornered men can.

Hakon, prompted by Cormac, shouted to them: "Ho, warriors, will ye listen to me?"

"We listen, Hakon," came back a shout from the barred windows, "but keep back; mayhap we be doomed men, but many shall die with us if you seek to take the skalli."

"I have no quarrel with you," answered Hakon. "I look upon you as friends, though you allowed Rognor to bind and imprison me. But that is past, let it be forgotten. Rognor is dead; his picked veterans are dead and ye have no leader. The forest about the steading swarms with Danes who but await my signal. But that signal I am loath to give. They will burn the skalli and cut the throats of every man, woman and child among you. Now attend me—if you will accept me as your chieftain, and swear fealty to me, no harm will come to you."

"What of the Danes?" came the shouted question. "Who are they that we should trust them?"

"You trust me, do you not? Have I ever broken my word?"

"No," they admitted, "you have always kept faith."

"Good enough. I swear to you that the Danes will not harm you. I have promised them a ship; that promise I must keep if they are to go in peace. But if you follow me on the Viking path, we can soon get another ship or build one. And one thing more—here stands beside me the girl who is to be my wife—the daughter of a British prince. She has promised me the aid of her people in all our endeavors. With friends on the British mainland we can have a source of supplies from whence we can raid the Angles and Saxons to our hearts' content—with the aid of Tarala's Britons we may carve us out a kingdom in Britain as Cerdic, Hengist and Horsa did. Now, speak—will you take me as your chief?"

A short silence followed in which the Vikings were evidently holding council with each other; then presently their spokesman shouted: "We agree to your wishes, O Hakon!"

Hakon laid down his notched and bloody sword and approached the skalli door empty-handed. "And will you swear fealty to me on the bull, the fire and the sword?"

The great portals swung open, framing fierce, bearded faces. "We will swear, Hakon; our swords are yours to command."

"And when they've found we've tricked them, they'll turn and cut his throat and ours," grunted Wulfhere, mopping the blood from his face.

Cormac smiled and shook his head. "They've sworn, they will keep faith. Are you badly wounded?"

"A trifle," growled the giant. "A gash in the thigh and a few more on the arms and shoulders. It was the cursed blood that got in my eyes when Rognor's sword bit through my helmet and into my scalp, as it broke. . . ."

"Your head's harder than your helmet, Wulfhere," laughed Cormac. "But here, we must be attending to our wounded. Some ten of our men are dead and nearly all of them slashed more or less. Also, some of the Jutes are down. But, by the gods, what a killing *we* have made this night!"

He indicated the stark and silent rows of arrow-feathered or sword-gashed Norsemen.

The sun, not yet in the zenith of the clear blue sky,

glimmered on the white sails of a long ship as they spread and swelled to catch the wind. On the deck stood a small group of figures.

Cormac extended his hand to Hakon. "We have hunted together well this night, young sir. A few hours since you were a captive doomed to die and Wulfhere and I were hunted outlaws. Now you are lord of Ladbhan and a band of hardy Vikings, and Wulfhere and I have a staunch ship under our feet—though forsooth, the crew is rather scant. Still, that can be overcome as soon as the Danes hear that Wulfhere and Cormac Mac Art need men.

"And you—" he turned to the girl who stood beside Hakon, still clad in the mail that hung loosely on her lithe form—"you are in truth a valkyrie—a shield woman. Your sons will be kings.'

"Aye, that they will," rumbled Wulfhere, enveloping Tarala's slim hand with his own huge paw. "Were I a marrying man, I might cut Hakon's throat and carry you off for myself. But now the wind is rising and my very heart quivers to feel the deck rocking under my feet again. Good fortune attend you all."

Hakon, his bride and the Norsemen attending them swung down into the boat that waited to carry them ashore. At Wulfhere's shout, his Danes cast off; the oars began to ply and the sails filled. The watchers in the boat and on shore saw the long-ship stand off.

"What now, old wolf?" roared Wulfhere, dealing Cormac a buffet between the shoulders that would have felled a horse. "Where away?—it is for you to say."

"To the Isle of Swords, first, for a full crew," the Gael answered, his eyes alight. "Then—" he drank in deeply the crisp strong tang of the seawind—"then, *skoal* for the Viking path again and the ends of the world!"

THE NIGHT OF THE WOLF

THE NIGHT OF THE WOLF

Thorwald Shield-hewer's gaze wandered from the glittering menace in the hard eyes of the man who fronted him, and strayed down the length of his great skalli. He marked the long lines of mailed, horn-helmed carles, the hawk-faced chiefs who had ceased feasting to listen. And Thorwald Shield-hewer laughed.

True, the man who had just flung his defiance into the Viking's teeth did not look particularly impressive beside the armored giants who thronged the hall. He was a short, heavily-muscled man, smooth-faced and very dark. His only garments or ornaments were rude sandals on his feet, a deerskin loincloth, and a broad leather girdle from which swung a short curiously-barbed sword. He wore no armor and his square-cut black mane was confined only by a thin silver band about his temples. His cold black eyes glittered with concentrated fury and his inner passions stirred the expressions of his usually immobile face.

"A year ago," said he, in barbarous Norse, "you came to Golara, desiring only peace with my people. You would be our friend and protect us from the raids of others of your accursed race. We were fools; we dreamed there was faith in a sea-thief. We listened. We brought you game and fish and cut timbers when

159

you built your steading, and shielded you from others of our people who were wiser than we. Then you were a handful with one long-ship. But as soon as your stockade was built, more of you came. Now your warriors number four hundred, and six dragon-ships are drawn up on the beach.

"Soon you became arrogant and overbearing. You insulted our chiefs, beat our young men—of late your devils have been carrying off our women and murdering our children and our warriors."

"And what would you have me do?" cynically asked Thorwald. "I have offered to pay your chief man-bote for each warrior slain causelessly by my carles. And as for your wenches and brats—a warrior should not trouble himself about such trifles."

"Man-bote!" the dark chief's eyes flashed in fierce anger. "Will silver wash out spilt blood? What is silver to we of the isles? Aye—the women of other races are trifles to you Vikings, I know. But you may find that dealing thus with the girls of the forest people is far from a trifle!"

"Well," broke in Thorwald sharply, "speak your mind and get hence. Your betters have more important affairs than listening to your clamor."

Though the other's eyes burned wolfishly, he made no reply to the insult.

"Go!" he answered, pointing seaward. "Back to Norge (Norway) or Hell or wherever you came from. If you will take your accursed presence hence, you may go in peace. I, Brulla, a chief of Hjaltland (Shetland Islands), have spoken."

Thorwald leaned back and laughed deeply; his comrades echoed his laughter and the smoky rafters shook with roars of jeering mirth.

"Why, you fool," sneered the Norseman, "do you think that Vikings ever let go of what they have taken hold? You Picts were fools enough to let us in—now we are the stronger. We of the North rule! Down on

your knees, fool, and thank the fates that we allow
you to live and serve us, rather than wiping out your
verminous tribe altogether! But henceforth ye shall
no longer be known as the Free People of Golara—
nay, ye shall wear the silver collar of thralldom and
men shall know ye as Thorwald's serfs!"

The Pict's face went livid and his self-control
vanished.

"Fool!" he snarled in a voice that rang through the
great hall like the grating of swords in battle. "You
have sealed your doom! You Norse rule all nations,
eh? Well, there be some who die, mayhap, but never
serve alien masters! Remember this, you blond swine,
when the forest comes to life about your walls and
you see your skalli crumble in flames and rivers of
blood! We of Golara were kings of the world in the
long ago when your ancestors ran with wolves in the
Arctic forests, and we do not bow the neck to such
as you! The hounds of Doom whine at your gates and
you shall die, Thorwald Shield-hewer, and you, Aslaf
Jarl's-bane, and you, Grimm Snorri's son, and you,
Osric, and you, Hakon Skel, and—" The Pict's finger,
stabbing at each of the flaxen-haired chiefs in turn,
wavered; the man who sat next to Hakon Skel differed
strangely from the others. Not that he was a whit less
wild and ferocious in his appearance. Indeed, with his
dark, scarred features and narrow, cold grey eyes, he
appeared more sinister than any of the rest. But he
was black-haired and clean-shaven, and his mail was
of the chain-mesh type forged by Irish armor-makers
instead of the scale-mail of the Norse. His helmet,
crested with flowing horse-hair, lay on the bench
beside him.

The Pict passed over him and ended with the pro-
nunciation of doom on the man beyond him—"And
you, Hordi Raven."

Aslaf Jarl's-bane, a tall, evil-visaged chief, leaped to
his feet: "Thor's blood, Thorwald, are we to listen to

the insolence of this jackal? I, who have been the death of a jarl in my day—"

Thorwald silenced him with a gesture. The sea-king was a yellow-bearded giant, whose eyes were those of a man used to rule. His every motion and intonation proclaimed the driving power, the ruthless strength of the man.

"You have talked much and loudly, Brulla," he said mildly. "Mayhap you are thirsty."

He extended a brimming drinking horn, and the Pict, thrown off guard by surprise, reached a mechanical hand for it, moving as if against his will. Then with a quick turn of his wrist, Thorwald dashed the contents full in his face. Brulla staggered with a cat-like scream of hellish fury, then his sword was out like a flash of summer lightning, and he bounded at his baiter. But his eyes were blinded by the stinging ale and Thorwald's quick-drawn sword parried his blind slashes while the Viking laughed mockingly. Then Aslaf caught up a bench and struck the Pict a terrible blow that stretched him stunned and bleeding at Thorwald's feet. Hakon Skel drew his dagger, but Thorwald halted him.

"I'll have no vermin's blood polluting my skalli floor. Ho, carles, drag this carrion forth."

The men-at-arms sprang forward with brutal eagerness. Brulla, half-senseless and bleeding, was struggling uncertainly to his knees, guided only by the wild beast fighting instinct of his race and his Age. They beat him down with shields, javelin shafts and the flat of axes, showering cruel blows on his defenseless body until he lay still. Then, jeering and jesting, they dragged him through the hall by the heels, arms trailing, and flung him contemptuously from the doorway with a kick and a curse. The Pictish chief lay face down and limply in the reddened dust, blood oozing from his pulped mouth—a symbol of the Viking's ruthless power.

Back at the feasting board, Thorwald drained a jack of foaming ale and laughed.

"I see that we must have a Pict-harrying," quoth he. "We must hunt these vermin out of the wood or they'll be stealing up in the night and loosing their shafts over the stockade."

"It will be a rare hunting!" cried Aslaf with an oath. "We cannot with honor fight such reptiles, but we can hunt them as we hunt wolves—"

"You and your vaporings of honor," sourly growled Grimm Snorri's son. Grimm was old, lean and cautious.

"You speak of honor and vermin," he sneered, "but the stroke of a maddened adder can slay a king. I tell you, Thorwald, you should have used more caution in dealing with these people. They outnumber us ten to one—"

"Naked and cowardly," replied Thorwald carelessly. "One Norseman is worth fifty such. And as for dealing with them, who is it that has been having his carles steal Pictish girls for him? Enough of your maunderings, Grimm. We have other matters to speak of."

Old Grimm muttered in his beard and Thorwald turned to the tall, powerfully-made stranger whose dark, inscrutable face had not altered during all the recent events. Thorwald's eyes narrowed slightly and a gleam came into them such as is seen in the eyes of a cat who plays with a mouse before devouring it.

"Partha Mac Othna," said he, playing with the name, "it is strange that so noted a reiver as you must be—though sooth to say, I never heard of your name before—comes to a strange steading in a small boat, alone."

"Not so strange as it would have been had I come with a boat-load of my blood-letters," answered the Gael. "Each of them has a half dozen blood feuds with the Norse. Had I brought them ashore, they and your carles would have been at each other's throats spite all you and I could do. But we, though we fight against each other at times, need not be such fools as to forego mutual advantage because of old rivalry."

"True, the Viking folk and the reivers of Ireland are not friends."

"And so, when my galley passed the lower tip of the island," continued the Gael, "I put out in the small boat, alone, with a flag of peace, and arrived here at sundown as you know. My galley continued to Makki Head, and will pick me up at the same point I left it, at dawn."

"So ho," mused Thorwald, chin on fist, "and that matter of my prisoner—speak more fully, Partha Mac Othna."

It seemed to the Gael that the Viking put undue accent on the name, but he answered: "Easy to say. My cousin Nial is captive among the Danes. My clan cannot pay the ransom they ask. It is no question of niggardliness—we have not the price they ask. But word came to us that in a sea-fight with the Danes off Helgoland you took a chief prisoner. I wish to buy him from you; we can use his captivity to force an exchange of prisoners with his tribe, perhaps."

"The Danes are ever at war with each other, Loki's curse on them. How know you but that my Dane is an enemy to they who hold your cousin?"

"So much the better," grinned the Gael. "A man will pay more to get a foe in his power than he will pay for the safety of a friend."

Thorwald toyed with his drinking horn. "True enough; you Gaels are crafty. What will you pay for this Dane—Hrut, he calls himself."

"Five hundred pieces of silver."

"His people would pay more."

"Possibly. Or perhaps not a piece of copper. It is a chance we are willing to take. Besides, it will mean a long sea voyage and risks taken to communicate with them. You may have the price I offer at dawn—

coin you never made more easily. My clan is not rich. The sea-kings of the North and the strong reivers of Erin have harried we lesser wolves to the edge of the seas. But a Dane we must have, and if you are too exorbitant, why we must sail eastward and take one by force of arms."

"That might be easy," mused Thorwald, "Dane-mark is torn by civil wars. Two kings contend against each other—or did, for I hear that Eric had the best of it, and Thorfinn fled the land."

"Aye—so the sea-wanderers say. Thorfinn was the better man, and beloved by the people, but Eric had the support of Jarl Anlaf, the most powerful man among the Danes, not even excepting the kings themselves."

"I heard that Thorfinn fled to the Jutes in a single ship, with a few followers," said Thorwald. "Would that I might have met that ship on the high seas! But this Hrut will serve. I would glut my hate for the Danes on a king, but I am content with the next noblest. And noble this man is, though he wears no title. I thought him a jarl at least, in the sea-fight, when my carles lay about him in a heap waist-high. Thor's blood, but he had a hungry sword! I made my wolves take him alive—but not for ransom. I might have wrung a greater price from his people than you offer, but more pleasant to me than the chink of gold, are the death groans of a Dane."

"I have told you," the Gael spread his hands help-lessly. "Five hundred pieces of silver, thirty golden torcs, ten Damascus swords we wrested from the brown men of Serkland (Barbary), and a suit of chain-mail armor I took from the body of a Frankish prince. More I cannot offer."

"Yet I can scarce forego the pleasure of carving the blood-eagle in the back of this Dane," murmured Thorwald, stroking his long, fair beard. "How will you pay this ransom—have you the silver and the rest in your garments?"

The Gael sensed the sneer in the tone, but paid no heed.

"Tomorrow at dawn you and I and the Dane will go to the lower point of the island. You may take ten men with you. While you remain on shore with the Dane, I will row out to my ship and bring back the silver and the rest, with ten of my own men. On the beach we will make the exchange. My men will remain in the boats and not even put foot ashore if you deal fairly with me."

"Well said," nodded Thorwald, as if pleased, yet the wolfish instinct of the Gael warned him that events were brewing. There was a gathering tension in the air. From the tail of his eye he saw the chiefs casually crowding near him. Grimm Snorri's son's lined, lean face was overcast and his hands twitched nervously. But no change in the Gael's manner showed that he sensed anything out of the ordinary.

"Yet it is but a poor price to pay for a man who will be the means of restoring a great Irish prince to his clan," Thorwald's tone had changed; he was openly baiting the other now, "besides I think I had rather carve the blood-eagle on his back after all—and on yours as well—*Cormac Mac Art!*"

He spat the last words as he straightened, and his chiefs surged about him. They were not an instant too soon. They knew by reputation the lightning-like coordination of the famous Irish pirate which made his keen brain realize and his steel thews act while an ordinary man would still be gaping. Before the words were fully out of Thorwald's mouth, Cormac was on him with a volcanic burst of motion that would have shamed a starving wolf. Only one thing saved the Shield-hewer's life; almost as quick as Cormac he flung himself backward off the feasting bench, and the Gael's flying sword killed a carle who stood behind it.

In an instant the flickering of swords made lightning in the smoky vastness of the skalli. It had been Cormac's intention to hack a swift way to the door and freedom, but he was hemmed too closely by blood-lusting warriors.

Scarcely had Thorwald crashed cursing to the floor, than Cormac wheeled back to parry the sword of Aslaf Jarl's bane who loomed over him like the shadow of Doom. The Gael's reddened blade turned Aslaf's stroke and before the Jarl slayer could regain his balance, death flooded his throat beneath Cormac's slicing point.

A backhand stroke shore through the neck-cords of a carle who was heaving up a great ax, and at the same instant Hordi Raven struck a blow that was intended to sever Cormac's shoulder bone. But the chain-mail turned the Raven's sword edge, and almost simultaneously Hordi was impaled on that glimmering point that seemed everywhere at once, weaving a web of death about the tall Gael. Hakon Skel, hacking at Cormac's unhelmed head, missed by a foot and received a slash across his face, but at that instant the Gael's feet became entangled with the corpses that littered the floor with shields and broken benches.

A concerted rush bore him back across the feasting board, where Thorwald hacked through his mail and gashed the ribs beneath. Cormac struck back desperately, shattering Thorwald's sword and beating the sea-king to his knees beneath the shock of the blow, but a club in the hands of a powerful carle crashed down on the Gael's unprotected head, laying the scalp open, and as he crumpled, Grimm Snorri's son struck the sword from his hand. Then, urged by Thorwald, the carles leaped upon him, smothering and crushing the half-senseless Reiver by sheer weight of manpower. Even so, their task was not easy, but at last they had torn the steel fingers from the bull throat of one of their number, about which they had blindly locked, and bound the Gael hand and foot with cords not even his dynamic strength could break. The carle he had half-strangled gasped on the floor as they dragged Cormac upright to face the sea-king who laughed in his face.

Cormac was a grim sight. He was red-stained by the blood both of himself and his foes, and from the gash in his scalp a crimson trickle seeped down to dry on his scarred face. But his wild beast vitality already asserted itself and there was no hint of a numbed brain in the cold eyes that returned Thorwald's domineering stare.

"Thor's blood!" swore the sea-king. "I'm glad your comrade Wulfhere Hausakliufr—the Skull-splitter—was not with you. I have heard of your prowess as a killer, but to appreciate it, one must see for himself. In the last three minutes I have seen more weapon-play than I have seen in battles that lasted hours. By Thor, you ranged through my carles like a hunger-maddened wolf through a flock of sheep! Are all your race like you?"

The Reiver deigned no reply.

"You are such a man as I would have for comrade," said Thorwald frankly. "I will forget all old feuds if you will join me." He spoke like a man who does not expect his wish to be granted.

Cormac's reply was merely a glimmer of cold scorn in his icy eyes.

"Well," said Thorwald, "I did not expect you to accede to my demand, and that spells your doom, because I cannot let such a foe to my race go free."

Then Thorwald laughed: "Your weapon-play has not been exaggerated but your craft has. You fool—to match wits with a Viking! I knew you as soon as I laid eyes on you, though I had not seen you in years. Where on the North Seas is such a man as you, with your height, shoulder-breadth—and scarred face? I had all prepared for you, before you had ceased telling me your first lie. Bah! A chief of Irish reivers. Aye—once, years ago. But now I know you for Cormac Mac Art *an Cliuin*, which is to say the Wolf, righthand man of Wulfhere Hausakliufr, a Viking of the Danes. Aye, Wulfhere Hausakliufr, hated of my race.

"You desired my prisoner Hrut to trade for your cousin! Bah! I know you of old, by reputation at least. And I saw you once, years ago—you came ashore with a lie on your lips to spy out my steading, to take report of my strength and weaknesses to Wulfhere, that you and he might steal upon me some night and burn the skalli over my head.

"Well, now you can tell me—how many ships has Wulfhere and where is he?"

Cormac merely laughed, a remarkably hard contemptuous laugh that enraged Thorwald. The sea-king's beard bristled and his eyes grew cruel.

"You will not answer me, eh?" he swore. "Well, it does not matter. Whether Wulfhere went on to Makki Head or not, three of my dragon-ships will be waiting for him off the Point at dawn. Then mayhap when I carve the blood-eagle on Hrut I will have Wulfhere's back also for my sport—and you may look on and see it well done, ere I hang you from the highest tree on Golara. To the cell with him!"

As the carles dragged Cormac away, the Gael heard the querulous, uneasy voice of Grimm Snorri's son raised in petulant dispute with his chief. Outside the door he noted, no limp body lay in the red-stained dust. Brulla had either recovered consciousness and staggered away, or been carried away by his tribesmen. These Picts were hard as cats to kill, Cormac knew, having fought their Caledonian cousins. A beating such as Brulla had received would have left the average man a crippled wreck, but the Pict would probably be fully recovered in a few hours, if no bones had been broken.

◆   ◆   ◆

Thorwald Shield-hewer's steading fronted on a small bay, on the beach of which were drawn up six long, lean ships, shield-railed and dragon-beaked. As was usual, the steading consisted of a great hall—the skalli—about which were grouped smaller buildings—stables, storehouses and the huts of the carles. Around the whole stretched a high stockade, built, like the houses, of heavy logs. The logs of the stockade were some ten feet high, set deep in the earth and sharpened on the top. There were loopholes here and there for arrows and at regularly-spaced intervals, shelves on the inner side on which the defenders might stand and strike down over the wall at the attackers. Beyond the stockade the tall dark forest loomed menacingly.

The stockade was in the form of a horseshoe with the open side seaward. The horns ran out into the shallow bay, protecting the dragon ships drawn up on the beach. An inner stockade ran straight across in front of the steading, from one horn to the other, separating the beach from the skalli. Men might swim out around the ends of the main stockade and gain the beach but they would still be blocked from the steading itself.

Thorwald's holdings seemed well protected, but vigilance was lax. Still, the Shetlands did not swarm with sea-rovers then as they did at a later date. The few Norse holdings there were like Thorwald's—mere pirate camps from which the Vikings swooped down on the Hebrides, the Orkneys and Britain, where the Saxons were trampling a fading Roman-Celtic civilization—and on Gaul, Spain and the Mediterranean.

Thorwald did not ordinarily expect a raid from the sea and Cormac had seen with what contempt the Vikings looked on the natives of the Shetlands. Wulfhere and his Danes were different; outlawed even among their own people, they ranged even farther than Thorwald himself, and they were keen-beaked birds of prey, whose talons tore all alike.

Cormac was dragged to a small hut built against the stockade at a point some distance from the skalli, and in this he was chained. The door slammed behind him and he was left to his meditations.

The Gael's shallow cuts had ceased to bleed, and inured to wounds—an iron man in an Age of iron—he gave them hardly a thought. Stung vanity bothered him; how easily he had slipped into Thorwald's trap, he whom kings had either cursed or blessed for his guile! Next time he would not be so over-confident, he mused; and a next time he was determined there should be. He did not worry overmuch about Wulfhere, even when he heard the shouts, scraping of slides and later the clack of oars that announced that three of Thorwald's long-ships were under way. Let them sneak to the Point and wait there till the dawn of Doom's Day! Neither he nor Wulfhere had been such utter fools as to trust themselves in the power of Thorwald's stronger force. Wulfhere had but one ship and some eighty men. They and the ship were even now hidden securely in a forest-screened cove on the other side of the island, which was less than a mile wide at this point. There was little chance of their being discovered by Thorwald's men and the risk of being spied out by some Pict was a chance that must be taken. If Wulfhere had followed their plan, he had run in after dark, feeling his way; there was no real reason why either Pict or Norseman should be lurking about. The shore about the cove was mainly wild, high cliffs, rugged and uninviting; moreover Cormac had heard that the Picts ordinarily avoided that part of the island because of some superstitious reason. There were ancient stone columns on the cliffs and a grim altar that hinted of ghastly rites in bygone ages.

Wulfhere would lurk there until Cormac returned to him, or until a smoke drifting up from the Point assured him that Thorwald was on hand with the prisoner and meaning no treachery. Cormac had carefully said nothing about the signal that was to bring Wulfhere, though he had not expected to be recognized for what he was. Thorwald had been wrong when he assumed that the prisoner had been used only for a blind. The Gael had lied about himself and about his reason for wishing the custody of Hrut, but it was true when he had said that it was news of the Dane's captivity that brought him to Golara.

Cormac heard the cautious oars die away in silence. He heard the clash of arms and the shouts of the carles. Then these noises faded, all but the steady tramp of sentries, guarding against a night attack.

It must be nearly midnight, Cormac decided, glancing up at the stars gleaming through his small heavily-barred window. He was chained close to the dirt floor and could not even rise to a sitting posture. His back was against the rear wall of the hut, which was formed by the stockade, and as he reclined there, he thought he heard a sound that was not of the sighing of the night-wind through the mighty trees without. Slowly he writhed about and found himself staring through a tiny aperture between two of the upright logs.

The moon had already set; in the dim starlight he could make out the vague outline of great, gently-waving branches against the black wall of the forest. Was there a subtle whispering and rustling among those shadows that was not of the wind and the leaves? Faint and intangible as the suggestion of nameless evil, the almost imperceptible noises ran the full length of the stockade. The whole night seemed full of ghostly murmurings—as if the midnight forest were stirring and moving its darksome self, like a shadowy monster coming to uncanny life. "When the forest comes to life," the Pict had said—

Cormac heard, within the stockade, one carle call to another. His rough voice reechoed in the whispering silence.

"Thor's blood, the trolls must be out tonight! How the wind whispers through the trees."

Even the dull-witted carle felt a hint of evil in the darkness and shadows. Gluing his eye to the crack, Cormac strove to pierce the darkness. The Gaelic pirate's faculties were as much keener than the average man's as a wolf's are keener than a hog's; his eyes were like a cat's in the dark. But in that utter blackness he could see nothing but the vague forms of the first fringe of trees. Wait!

Something took shape in the shadows. A long line of figures moved like ghosts just under the shadows of the trees; a shiver passed along Cormac's spine. Surely these creatures were elves, evil demons of the forest. Short and mightily built, half stooping, one behind the other, they passed in almost utter silence. In the shadows their silence and their crouching positions made them monstrous travesties on men. Racial memories, half lost in the misty gulfs of consciousness, came stealing back to claw with icy fingers at Cormac's heart. He did not fear them as a man fears a human foe; it was the horror of world-old, ancestral memories that gripped him—dim felt, chaotic dream-recollections of darker Ages and grimmer days when primitive men battled for supremacy in a new world.

For these Picts were a remnant of a lost tribe—the survivals of an elder epoch—last outposts of a dark Stone Age empire that crumbled before the bronze swords of the first Celts. Now these survivors, thrust out on the naked edges of the world they had once ruled, battled grimly for their existence.

There could be no accurate counting of them because of the darkness and the swiftness of their slinking gait, but Cormac reckoned that at least four hundred passed his line of vision. That band alone was equal to Thorwald's full strength and far outnumbered the men left in the steading now, since Thorwald had sent out three of his ships. The skulking

figures passed as they had come, soundless, leaving
no trace behind, like ghosts of the night.

Cormac waited in a silence that had become suddenly tense. Then without warning the night was shattered by one fearful death-yell! Pandemonium broke
loose and a mad hell of sound burst on the air. And
now the forest came to life! From all sides stocky
figures broke cover and swarmed on the barricades.
A lurid glare shed a ghastly light over all and Cormac
tore savagely at his chains, wild with excitement. Monstrous events were occurring without, and here he
was, chained like a sheep for the slaughter! He
cursed incredibly.

The Norsemen were holding the wall; the clash of
steel rose deafeningly in the night, the hum of arrows
filled the air, and the deep fierce shouts of the Vikings
vied with the hellish wolf-howling of the Picts. Cormac could not see, but he sensed the surging of
human waves against the stockade, the plying of
spears and axes, the reeling retreat and the renewed
onset. The Picts, he knew, were without mail and
indifferently armed. It was very possible that the limited force of Vikings could hold the stockade until
Thorwald returned with the rest, as he would assuredly
do when he saw the flame—but whence came the
flame?

Someone was fumbling at the door. It swung open
and Cormac saw the lean shambling frame and livid
bearded face of Grimm Snorri's son limned against
the red glare. In one hand he held a helmet and a
sword Cormac recognized as his own, in the other a
bunch of keys which jangled as his hand shook.

"We are all dead men!" squawked the old Viking,
"I warned Thorwald! The woods are alive with Picts!
There are thousands of them! We can never hold the
stockade until Thorwald returns! He is doomed too,
for the Picts will cut him off when he comes into the
bay and feather his men with arrows before they can

come to grips! They have swum around the outer horns of the stockade and set the three remaining galleys on fire! Osric would run like a fool with a dozen carles to save the ships and he had scarcely gotten outside the gates before he was down with a score of black shafts through him and his men were cut off and hemmed in by a hundred howling demons! Not a man of them escaped, and we barely had time to shut the gates when the whole screaming mob was battering at them!

"We have slain them by the scores, but for every one that drops, three spring to take his place. I have seen more Picts tonight than I knew were on Golara—or in the world. Cormac, you are a bold man; you have a ship somewhere off the isle—swear to save me and I will set you free! Mayhap the Picts will not harm you—that devil Brulla did not name you in his death rune.

"If any man can save me it is you! I will show you where Hrut is hidden and we'll take him with us—" he threw a quick glance over his shoulder toward the roar of battle beachward, and went white. "Thor's blood!" he screamed, "The gates have given way and the Picts are inside the inner stockade!"

The howling rose to a crescendo of demoniac passion and fiendish exultation.

"Loose me, you gibbering fool!" raged Cormac, tearing at his chains. "You've time enough for babbling when—"

Chattering with fear, Grimm Snorri's son stepped inside the hut, fumbling with the keys—even as his foot crossed the threshold a lean shape raced swift and silent as a wolf out of the flame-shot shadows. A dark arm hooked about the old Viking's withered neck, jerking his chin up. One fearful shriek burst from his writhing lips to break short in a ghastly gurgle as a keen edge whipped across his leathery throat.

Over the twitching corpse of his victim, the Pict

eyed Cormac Mac Art, and the Gael stared back, expecting death, but unafraid. Then in the glare of the burning ships, that made the cell-hut as light as day, Cormac saw that the slayer was the chief, Brulla.

"You are he who slew Aslaf and Hordi. I watched through the door of the skalli before I dragged myself away to the forests," said the Pict, as calmly as though no inferno of combat was raging without, "I told my people of you and warned them not to harm you, if you still lived. You hate Thorwald as well as I. I will free you; glut your vengeance; soon will Thorwald return in his ships and we will cut his throat. There shall be no more Norse or Golara. All the free people of the isles here-abouts are gathering to aid us, and Thorwald is doomed!"

He bent over the Gael and released him. Cormac sprang erect, a fresh fire of confidence surging through his veins. He snatched his helmet with its flowing horsehair crest, and his long straight sword. He also took the keys from Brulla.

"Know you where was prisoned the Dane called Hrut?" he asked, as they stepped through the door. Brulla pointed across a seething whirlpool of flame and hacking swords.

"The smoke obscures the hut at present, but it lies next the storehouse on that side."

Cormac nodded and set off at a run. Where Brulla went he neither knew nor cared. The Picts had fired stable, storehouse and skalli, as well as the ships on the beach outside the inner stockade. About the skalli and here and there close to the stockade which was also burning in a score of places, stubborn fighting went on, as the handful of survivors sold their lives with all the desperate ferocity of their breed. There were, indeed, thousands of the short, dark men, who swarmed about each tall blond warrior in a slashing, hammering mass. The heavy swords of the mailed Vikings took fearful toll, but the smaller men lashed in with a wild beast frenzy that made naught of wounds, and pulled down their giant foes by sheet weight of numbers. Once on the ground, the stabbing swords of the dark men did their work. Screams of death and yells of fury rent the flame-reddened skies, but as Cormac ran swiftly toward the storehouse, he heard no pleas for mercy. Driven to madness by countless outrages, the Picts were glutting their vengeance to the uttermost, and the Norse people neither looked nor asked for mercy.

Blond-haired women, cursing and spitting in the faces of their killers, felt the knife jerked across their white throats, and Norse babes were butchered with no more compunction than their sires had shown in the slaughter—for sport—of Pictish infants.

Cormac took no part in this holocaust. None of these people was his friend—either race would cut his throat if the chance arose. As he ran he used his sword merely to parry chance cuts that fell on him from Pict and Norseman alike, and so swiftly he moved between staggering clumps of gasping, slashing men, that he ran his way across the open space without serious opposition. He reached the hut and a few seconds' work with the lock opened the heavy door. He had not come too soon; sparks from the burning storehouse nearby had caught on the hut thatch and already the interior was full of smoke. Through this Cormac groped his way toward a figure he could barely make out in the corner. There was a jangling of chains and a voice with a Danish accent spoke: "Slay me, in the name of Loki; better a sword thrust than this accursed smoke!"

Cormac knelt and fumbled at his chains. "I come to free you, O Hrut," he gasped. A moment later he dragged the astonished warrior to his feet and together they staggered out of the hut, just as the roof fell in. Drawing in great draughts of air, Cormac turned and stared curiously at his companion—a splendid, red-maned giant of a man, with the bearing of a noble. He was half-naked, ragged and unkempt from weeks of captivity, but his eyes gleamed with an unconquerable light.

"A sword!" he cried, those eyes blazing as they swept the scene, "A sword, good sir, in the name of Thor! Here is a goodly brawl and we stand idle!"

Cormac stooped and tore a reddened blade from the stiffening hand of an arrow-feathered Norseman.

"Here is a sword, Hrut," he growled, "but for whom will you strike—the Norse who have kept you cooped like a caged wolf and would have slain you— or the Picts who will cut your throat because of the color of your hair?"

"There can be but little choice," answered the Dane. "I heard the screams of women—"

"The women are all dead," grunted the Gael. "We cannot help them now; we must save ourselves. It is the night of the wolf—and the wolves are biting!"

"I would like to cross swords with Thorwald," the big Dane hesitated as Cormac drew him toward the flaming barrier.

"Not now, not now," the reiver rasped, "bigger game is afoot, Thor—Hrut! Later we will come back and finish what the Picts leave—just now we have more than ourselves to think about, for if I know Wulfhere Skull-splitter he is already marching through the woods at double-quick time!"

The stockade was in places a smoldering mass of coals; Cormac and his companion battered a way through and even as they stepped into the shadows of the trees outside, three figures rose about them and set upon them with bestial howls. Cormac shouted a warning, but it was useless. A whirling blade was at his throat and he had to strike to save himself. Turning from the corpse he had been loath to make, he saw Hrut, bestriding the mangled body of one Pict,

take the barbed sword of the other in his left arm
and split the wielder's skull with an overhand stroke.

Cursing, the Gael sprang forward. "Are you badly
hurt?" Blood was gushing from a deep wound in
Hrut's mighty arm.

"A scratch," the Dane's eyes blazed with the battle-
light. But despite his protests Cormac tore a strip
from his 'own garments and bound the arm so as to
staunch the flow of blood.

"Here, help me drag these bodies under the
brush," growled the reiver. "I hated to strike—but
when they saw your red beard it was our lives or
theirs. I think Brulla would see our point of view, but
if the rest find we killed their brothers neither Brulla
nor the devil can keep their swords from our throats."

This done—"Listen!" commanded Hrut. The roar
of battle had dwindled in the main to a crackle and
roar of flames and the hideous and triumphant yelling
of the Picts. Only in a single room in the flaming
skalli, yet untouched by the fire, a handful of Vikings
still kept up a stubborn defense. Through the noise
of the fire there sounded a rhythmic clack-clack-clack!

"Thorwald is returning!" exclaimed Cormac, springing back to the edge of the forest to peer over the
ruins of the stockade. Into the bay swept a single
dragon-ship. The long ash oars drove her plunging
through the water and from her rowers and from the
men massed on poop and gunwale rose a roar of
deep-toned ferocity as they saw the smoking ruins of
the steading and the mangled bodies of their people.
From the burning skalli came an echoing shout. In
the smoldering glare that turned the bay to a gulf of
blood, Cormac and Hrut saw the hawk-face of Hakon
Skel where he stood on the poop. But where were
the other two ships? Cormac thought he knew and a
smile of grim appreciation crossed his somber face.

Now the dragon-ship was sweeping in to the beach
and hundreds of screaming Picts were wading out to

meet it. Waist deep in water, holding their heavy black bows high to keep the cords dry, they loosed their arrows and a storm of shafts swept the dragon-ship from stem to stern. Full into the teeth of the deadliest gale it had ever faced the dragon-ship drove, while men went down in windrows along the gun-wales, transfixed by the long black shafts that rent through lindenwood buckler and scale mail armor to pierce the flesh beneath.

The rest crouched behind their shields and rowed and steered as best they could. Now the keel grated on the water-flooded sand and the swarming savages closed about her. By the hundreds they scrambled up the sides, the stern and the arching prow, while others maintained a steady fire from the water and the beach. Their marksmanship was almost uncanny. Flying between two slashing Picts a long shaft would strike down a Norseman. But when it came to hand-grips, the advantage was immensely with the Vikings. Their giant stature, their armor and long swords, and their position on the gunwales above their foes made them for the moment invincible.

Swords and axes rose and fell, spattering blood and brains, and stocky shapes dropped writhing from the sides of the galley to sink like stones. The water about the ship grew thick with dead, and Cormac caught his breath as he realized the lavishness with which the naked Picts were spending their lives. But soon he heard their chiefs shouting to them and he realized, as the attackers drew sullenly away, that their leaders were shouting for them to fall back and pick off the Vikings at long range.

The Vikings soon realized that also. Hakon Skel dropped with an arrow through his brain and with yells of fury the Norsemen began leaping from their ship into the water, in one desperate attempt to close with their foes and take toll in death. The Picts accepted the challenge. About each Norseman closed a dozen Picts and the bay along the beach seethed and eddied with battle. The waves grew red as blood and corpses floated thick or littered the bottom, tripping the feet and clogging the arms of the living. The warriors penned in the skalli sallied forth to die with their tribesmen.

Then what Cormac had looked for, occurred. A deep-chested roar thundered above the fury of the fight, and from the woods that fringed the bay burst Thorwald Shield-hewer, with the crews of two dragonships at his back. Cormac knew that, guessing what had occurred, he had sent the other ship on to draw the Picts out and give him time to land below the bay and march through the forest with the rest of his men.

Now in a solid formation, shield locking shield, they swept from the woods along the shore and bore down the beach toward their foes. With howls of unquenchable fury, the Picts turned on them with a rain of shafts and a headlong charge of stocky bodies and stabbing blades. But the arrows in the main glanced from the close-lapping shields and the mob-like rush met a solid wall of iron. But with the same desperation they had shown all during the fight, the Picts hurled charge after charge on the shield-wall. It was a living sea that broke in red waves on that iron bulwark. The ground grew thick under foot with corpses, not all Pictish. But as often as a Norseman fell, his comrades locked their great shields close as ever, trampling the fallen under foot. No longer did the Vikings surge forward, but they stood like a solid rock and took not a single backward step. The wings of their wedge-shaped formation were forced inward as the Picts entirely surrounded them, until it was more like a square, facing all ways. And like a square of stone and iron it stood, and all the wild, blind charges of the Picts failed to shake it, though they hurled their bare breasts against the steel until their corpses formed a wall over which the living clambered.

Then suddenly, apparently without warning, they broke and fled in all directions, some across the flame-lit space of the steading, some into the forest. With yells of triumph the Vikings broke formation and plunged after them, though Cormac saw Thorwald screaming frantic orders and beating at his men with the flat of his reddened sword. A trick! Cormac knew it as well as Thorwald but the blind fighting frenzy of the carles betrayed them as their foes had guessed. The moment they streamed out loosely in pursuit, the Picts turned howling and a dozen Vikings went down before a hail of arrows. Before the rest could reform their position they were surrounded singly and in struggling clumps, and the work of death began. From a single massed battle, the combat became a score of single skirmishes on the beach—where the survivors of the dragon-ship had made their way—before the skalli's embers and in the fringe of the forest.

And suddenly as from a dream Cormac woke and cursed himself.

"By the blood of the gods, what a fool I am! Are we boys who have never seen a battle, to stand here gaping when we should be legging it through the forest?"

He was forced to fairly drag Hrut away, and the two ran swiftly through the forest, hearing on all sides the clangor of arms and the shouts of death. The battle had spilled over into the forest and that grim and darksome wood was the scene of many a bloody deed. But Cormac and Hrut, warned by the sounds, managed to keep clear of such struggles, though once vague figures leaped at them from the shadows, and in the blind brief whirl of battle that followed, they never knew whether it was Picts or Norsemen who fell before their swords.

Then the sounds of conflict were behind them and in front sounded the tramp of many men. Hrut stopped short, gripping his red-stained sword, but Cormac pulled him on.

"Men marching in time; they can be none but Wulfhere's wolves!"

The next instant they burst into a glade, dimly lighted by the first whiteness of dawn, and from the opposite side strode a band of red-bearded giants, whose chief, looking like a very god of war, bellowed a welcome:

"Cormac! Thor's blood, it seems we've been marching through these accursed woods forever! When I saw the glow above the trees and heard the yelling I brought every carle on the ship, for I knew not but what you were burning and looting Thorwald's steading single handed! What is forward—and who is this?"

"This is Hrut—whom we sought," answered Cormac. "Hell and the red whirlpools of war are what is forward—there's blood on your axe!"

"Aye—we had to hack our way through a swarm of small, dark fellows—Picts I believe you call 'em."

Cormac cursed. "We'll pile up a blood-score that even Brulla can't answer for—"

"Well," grumbled the giant, "the woods are full of them, and we heard them howling like wolves behind us—"

"I had thought all would be at the steading," commented Hrut.

Cormac shook his head. "Brulla spoke of a gathering of clans; they have come from all the isles of the Hjaltlands and probably landed on all sides of the island—listen!"

The clamor of battle grew louder as the fighters penetrated deeper into the mazes of the forest, but from the way Wulfhere and his Vikings had come there sounded a long-drawn yell like a pack of running wolves, swiftly rising higher and higher.

"Close ranks!" yelled Cormac, paling, and the

Danes had barely time to lock their shields before the pack was upon them. Bursting from the thick trees a hundred Picts whose swords were yet unstained broke like a tidal wave on the shields of the Danes.

Cormac, thrusting and slashing like a fiend, shouted to Wulfhere: "Hold them hard—I must find Brulla. He will tell them we are foes of Thorwald and allow us to depart in peace!"

All but a handful of the original attackers were down, trodden under foot and snarling in their death throes. Cormac leaped from the shelter of the overlapping shields and darted into the forest. Searching for the Pictish chief in that battle-tortured forest was little short of madness, but it was their one lone chance. Seeing the fresh Picts coming up from behind them had told Cormac that he and his comrades would probably have to fight their way across the whole island to regain their galley. Doubtless these were warriors from some island lying to the east, who had just landed on Golara's eastern coast.

If he could find Brulla—he had not gone a score of paces past the glade when he stumbled over two corpses, locked in a death-grapple. One was Thorwald Shield-hewer. The other was Brulla. Cormac stared at them and as the wolf-yell of the Picts rose about him, his skin crawled. Then he sprang up and ran back to the glade where he had left the Danes.

Wulfhere leaned on his great ax and stared at the corpses at his feet. His men stolidly held their position.

"Brulla is dead," snapped the Gael. "We must aid ourselves. These Picts will cut our throats if they can, and the gods know they have no cause to love a Viking. Our only chance is to get back to our ship if we can. But that is a slim chance indeed, for I doubt not but that the woods are full of the savages. We can never keep the shield-wall position among the trees, but—"

"Think of another plan, Cormac," said Wulfhere grimly, pointing to the east with his great axe. There a lurid glow was visible among the trees and a hideous medley of howling came faintly to their ears. There was but one answer to that red glare.

"They've found and fired our ship," muttered Cormac. "By the blood of the gods, Fate's dice are loaded against us."

Suddenly a thought came to him.

"After me! Keep close together and hew your way through, if needs be, but follow me close!"

Without question they followed him through the corpse-strewn forest, hearing on each hand the sound of fighting men, until they stood at the forest fringe and gazed over the crumbled stockade at the ruins of the steading. By merest chance no body of Picts had opposed their swift march, but behind them rose a frightful and vengeful clamor as a band of them came upon the corpse-littered glade the Danes had just left.

No fighting was going on among the steading's ruins. The only Norsemen in sight were mangled corpses. The fighting had swept back into the forest whither the close-pressed Vikings had retreated or been driven. From the incessant clashing of steel within its depths, those who yet remained alive were giving a good account of themselves. Under the trees where bows were more or less useless, the survivors might defend themselves for hours, though, with the island swarming with Picts, their ultimate fate was certain.

Three or four hundred tribesmen, weary of battle at last, had left the fighting to their fresher tribesmen and were salvaging what loot they could from the embers of the storehouses.

"Look!" Cormac's sword pointed to the dragon-ship whose prow, driven in the sands, held her grounded, though her stern was afloat. "In a moment we will have a thousand yelling demons on our backs. There lies our one chance, wolves—Hakon Skel's *Raven*. We must hack through and gain it, shove it free and row off before the Picts can stop us. Some of us will die, and we may all die, but it's our only chance!"

The Vikings said nothing, but their fierce light eyes blazed and many grinned wolfishly. Touch and go! Life or death on the toss of the dice! That was a Viking's only excuse for living!

"Lock shields!" roared Wulfhere. "Close ranks! The flying-wedge formation—Hrut in the center."

"What—!" began Hrut angrily, but Cormac shoved him unceremoniously between the mailed ranks.

"You have no armor," he growled impatiently. "Ready old wolf? Then charge, and the gods choose the winners!"

Like an avalanche the steel-tipped wedge shot from the trees and raced toward the beach. The Picts looting the ruins turned with howls of amazement, and a straggling line barred the way to the water's edge. But without slacking gait the flying shield-wall struck the Pictish line, buckled it, crumpled it, hacked it down and trampled it under, and over its red ruins rushed upon the beach.

Here the formation was unavoidably broken. Waist-deep in water, tripping among corpses, harried by the rain of arrows that now poured upon them from the beach, the Vikings gained the dragon-ship and swarmed up its sides, while a dozen giants set their shoulders against the prow to push it off the sands. Half of them died in the attempt, but the titanic efforts of the rest triumphed and the galley began to give way.

The Danes were the bowmen among the Viking races. Thirty of the eighty-odd warriors who followed Wulfhere wore heavy bows and quivers of long arrows strapped to their backs. As many of these as could be spared from oars and sweeps now unslung their weapons and directed their shafts on the Picts wading into the water to attack the men at the prow. In the first light of the rising sun the Danish shafts did fearful execution, and the advance wavered and fell back. Arrows fell all about the craft and some found their marks, but crouching beneath their shields the warriors toiled mightily, and soon, though it seemed like hours, the dragon-ship rolled and wallowed free, the men in the water leaped and caught at chains and gunwale, and the long oars drove her out into the bay, just as a howling horde of wolfish figures swept out of the woods and down the beach. Their arrows fell in a rain, rattling harmlessly from shield-rail and hull as the *Raven* shot toward the open sea.

"Touch and go!" roared Wulfhere with a great laugh, smiting Cormac terrifically between the shoulders. Hrut shook his head. To his humiliated anger, a big carle had been told off to keep a shield over him, during the fight.

"Many brave warriors are dying in yonder woods. It pains me to desert them thus, though they are our foes and would have put me to death."

Cormac shrugged his shoulders. "I, too, would have aided them had I seen a way. But we could have accomplished naught by remaining and dying with them. By the blood of the gods, what a night this has been! Golara is rid of her Vikings, but the Picts paid a red price! All of Thorwald's four hundred are dead now or soon will be, but not less than a thousand Picts have died outright in the steading and the gods only know how many more in the forest."

Wulfhere glanced at Hrut where he stood on the poop, outstretched hand on the sword whose reddened point rested on the deal planking. Unkempt, bloodstained, tattered, wounded, yet still his kingly carriage was unabated.

"And now that you have rescued me so boldly against incredible odds," said he, "what would you have of me besides my eternal gratitude, which you already have?"

Wulfhere did not reply; turning to the men who rested on their oars to gaze eagerly and expectantly up at the group on the poop, the Viking chief lifted his red axe and bellowed: "Skoal, wolves! Yell hail for Thorfinn Eagle-crest, king of Dane-mark!"

A thunderous roar went up to the blue of the morning skies that startled the wheeling sea gulls. The tattered king gasped in amazement, glancing quickly from one to the other, not yet certain of his status.

"And now that you have recognized me," said he, "am I guest or prisoner?"

Cormac grinned. "We traced you from Skagen, whence you fled in a single ship to Helgoland, and learned there that Thorwald Shield-hewer had taken captive a Dane with the bearing of a king. Knowing you would conceal your identity, we did not expect him to know that he had a king of the Danes in his hands.

"Well, King Thorfinn, this ship and our swords are yours. We be outlaws, both from our own lands. You cannot alter my status in Erin, but you can inlaw Wulfhere and make Danish ports free to us."

"Gladly would I do this, my friends," said Thorfinn, deeply moved. "But how can I aid my friends, who cannot aid myself? I, too, am an outcast, and my cousin Eric rules the Danes."

"Only until we set foot on Danish soil!" exclaimed Cormac. "Oh, Thorfinn, you fled too soon, but who can foresee the future? Even as you put to sea like a hunted pirate, the throne was rocking under Eric's feet. While you lay captive on Thorwald's dragon-ship, Jarl Anlaf fell in battle with the Jutes and Eric lost his greatest supporter. Without Anlaf, his rule will crumble overnight and hosts will flock to your banner!"

Thorfinn's eyes lighted with a wondrous gleam. He

threw his head back as a lion throws back his mane and flung up his reddened sword into the eye of the rising sun.

"Skoal!" he cried. "Head for Dane-mark, my friends, and may Thor fill our sail!"

"Aim her prow eastward, carles," roared Wulfhere to the men at the sweeps. "We go to set a new king on the throne of Dane-mark!"

THE TEMPLE OF ABOMINATION

THE TEMPLE OF ABOMINATION

"Easy all," grunted Wulfhere Hausakliufr. "I see the glimmer of a stone building through the trees. . . . Thor's blood, Cormac! are you leading us into a trap?"

The tall Gael shook his head, a frown darkening his sinister, scarred face.

"I never heard of a castle in these parts; the British tribes hereabouts don't build in stone. It may be an old Roman ruin—"

Wulfhere hesitated, glancing back at the compact lines of bearded, horn-helmeted warriors. "Maybe we'd best send out a scout."

Cormac Mac Art laughed jeeringly. "Alaric led his Goths through the Forum over eighty years ago, yet you barbarians still start at the name of Rome. Fear not; there are no legions in Britain. I think this is a Druidic temple. We have nothing to fear from them— more especially as we are moving against their hereditary enemies."

"And Cerdic's brood will howl like wolves when we strike them from the west instead of the south or east," said the Skull-splitter with a grin. "It was a crafty idea of yours, Cormac, to hide our dragon-ship on the west coast and march straight through British country to fall on the Saxons. But it's mad, too."

"There's method in my madness," responded the Gael. "I know that there are few warriors hereabouts; most of the chiefs are gathering about Arthur Pendragon for a great concerted drive. Pendragon—ha! He's no more Uther Pendragon's son than you are. Uther was a black-bearded madman—more Roman than Briton and more Gaul than Roman. Arthur is as fair as Eric there. And he's pure Celt—a waif from one of the wild western tribes that never bowed to Rome. It was Lancelot who put it into his head to make himself king—else he had still been no more than a wild chief raiding the borders."

"Has he become smooth and polished like the Romans were?"

"Arthur? Ha! One of your Danes might seem a gentlewoman beside him. He's a shock-headed savage with a love for battle." Cormac grinned ferociously and touched his scars. "By the blood of the gods, he has a hungry sword! It's little gain we reivers from Erin have gotten on his coasts!"

"Would I could cross steel with him," grunted Wulfhere, thumbing the flaring edge of his great axe. "What of Lancelot?"

"A renegade Gallo-Roman who has made an art of throat-cutting. He varies reading Petronius with plotting and intriguing. Gawaine is a pure-blooded Briton like Arthur, but he has Romanish leanings. You'd laugh to see him aping Lancelot—but he fights like a blood-hungry devil. Without these two, Arthur would have been no more than a bandit chief. He can neither read nor write."

"What of that?" rumbled the Dane. "Neither can I. . . . Look—there's the temple."

They had entered the tall grove in whose shadows crouched the broad, squat building that seemed to leer out at them from behind a screening row of columns.

"This can be no temple of the Britons," growled

Wulfhere. "I thought they were mostly of a sickly new sect called Christians."

"The Roman-British mongrels are," said Cormac. "The pure Celts hold to the old gods, as do we of Erin. By the blood of the gods, we Gaels will never turn Christian while one Druid lives!"

"What do these Christians?" asked Wulfhere curiously.

"They eat babies during their ceremonies, it is said."

"But 'tis also said the Druids burn men in cages of green wood."

"A lie spread by Caesar and believed by fools!" rasped Cormac impatiently. "I laud not the Druids especially, but wisdom of the elements and ages is not denied to them. These Christians teach meekness and the bowing of the neck to the blow."

"What say you?" The great Viking was sincerely amazed. "Is it truly their creed to take blows like slaves?"

"Aye—to return good for evil and to forgive their oppressors."

The giant meditated on this statement for a moment. "That is not a creed, but cowardice," he decided finally. "These Christians be all madmen. Cormac, if you recognize one of that breed, point him out and I will try his faith." He lifted his axe meaningfully. "For look you," he said, "that is an insidious and dangerous teaching which may spread like rust on the wheat and undermine the manhood of men if it be not stamped out like a young serpent under heel."

"Let me but see one of these madmen," said Cormac grimly, "and I will begin the stamping. But let us see to this temple. Wait here—I'm of the same belief as these Britons, if I am of a different race. These Druids will bless our raid against the Saxons.

Much is mummery, but their friendship at least is desirable."

The Gael strode between the columns and vanished. The Hausakliufr leaned on his axe; it seemed to him that from within came a faint rattle—like the hoofs of a goat on a marble floor.

"This is an evil place," muttered Osric Jarl's-bane. "I thought I saw a strange face peering about the top of the column a moment agone."

"It was a fungus vine grown and twisted about," Black Hrothgar contradicted him. "See how the fungus springs up all about the temple—how it twists and writhes like souls in torment—how human-like is its appearance—"

"You are both mad," broke in Hakon Shorri's son. "It was a goat you saw—I saw the horns that grew upon its head—"

"Thor's blood," snarled Wulfhere, "be silent—listen!"

Within the temple had sounded the echo of a sharp, incredulous cry; a sudden, demonic rapping as of fantastic hoofs on marble flags; the rasp of a sword from its scabbard, and a heavy blow. Wulfhere gripped his axe and took the first step of a headlong charge for the portals. Then from between the columns, in silent haste, came Cormac Mac Art. Wulfhere's eyes widened and a slow horror crept over him, for never till this moment had he seen the steel nerves of the lean Gael shaken—yet now the color was gone from Cormac's face and his eyes stared like those of a man who has looked into dark, nameless gulfs. His blade dripped red.

"What in the name of Thor—?" growled Wulfhere, peering fearfully into the shadow-haunted shrine.

Cormac wiped away beads of cold sweat and moistened his lips.

"By the blood of the gods," he said, "we have stumbled upon an abomination—or else I am mad! From the inner gloom it came bounding and capering—suddenly—and it almost had me in its grasp before I had sense enough to draw and strike. It leaped and capered like a goat, but ran upright—and in the dim light it was not unlike a man."

"You are mad," said Wulfhere uneasily; his mythology did not include satyrs.

"Well," snapped Cormac, "the thing lies upon the flags within; follow me, and I will prove to you whether I am mad."

He turned and strode through the columns, and Wulfhere followed, axe ready, his Vikings trailing behind him in close formation and going warily. They passed between the columns, which were plain and without ornamentation of any kind, and entered the temple. Here they found themselves within a broad hall flanked with squat pillars of black stone—and these indeed were carved. A squat figure squatted on the top of each, as upon a pedestal, but in the dim light it was impossible to make out what sort of beings these figures represented, though there was an abhorrent hint of abnormality about each shape.

"Well," said Wulfhere impatiently, "where is your monster?"

"There he fell," said Cormac, pointing with his sword, "and—by the black gods!"

The flags lay bare.

"Moon-mist and madness," said Wulfhere, shaking his head. "Celtic superstition. You see ghosts, Cormac!"

"Yes?" snapped the badgered Gael. "Who saw a troll on the beacon of Helgoland and roused the whole camp with shouts and bellowings? Who kept the band under arms all night and kept men feeding the fires till they nearly dropped, to scare away the things of darkness?"

Wulfhere growled uncomfortably and glared at his warriors as if to challenge anyone to laugh.

"Look," said Cormac, bending closer. On the tiling was a wide smear of blood, freshly spilt. Wulfhere took a single glance and then straightened quickly, glaring into the shadows. His men bunched closer, facing outward, beards a-bristle. A tense silence reigned.

"Follow me," said Cormac in a low tone, and they pressed close at his heels as he walked warily down the broad corridor. Apparently no entrance opened between the brooding, evil pillars. Ahead of them the shadows paled and they came forth into a broad circular chamber with a domed ceiling. Around this chamber were more pillars, regularly spaced, and in the light that flowed somehow through the dome the warriors saw the nature of those pillars and the shapes that crowned them. Cormac swore between his teeth and Wulfhere spat. The figures were human, and not even the most perverse and degenerate geniuses of decadent Greece and later Rome could have conceived such obscenities or breathed into the tortured stone such foul life. Cormac scowled. Here and there in the sculpturing the unknown artists had struck a cord of unrealness—a hint of abnormality beyond any human deformity. These touches roused in him a vague uneasiness, a crawling, shuddersome half-fear that lurked white-maned and grisly at the back of his mind . . .

The thought that he had briefly entertained, that he had seen and slain an hallucination, vanished.

Besides the doorway through which they had entered the chamber, four other portals showed—narrow, arched doorways, apparently without doors. There was no altar visible. Cormac strode to the center of the dome and looked up; its shadowy hollow arched above him, sullen and brooding. His gaze sought the floor on which he stood and he noted the pattern—of tiling rather than flags, and laid in a design the lines of which converged to the center of the floor. The focus of that design was a single, broad, octagonal slab on which he was standing . . .

Then, even as he realized that he was standing on that slab, it fell away silently from under his feet and he felt himself plunging into an abyss beneath.

Only the Gael's superhuman quickness saved him. Thorfinn Jarl's-bane was standing nearest him and, as the Gael dropped, he shot out a long arm and clutched at the Dane's sword-belt. The desperate fingers missed, but closed on the scabbard—and, as Thorfinn instinctively braced his legs, Cormac's fall was checked and he swung suspended, life hanging on the grip of his single hand and the strength of the scabbard loops. In an instant Thorfinn had seized his wrist, and Wulfhere, leaping forward with a roar of alarm, added the grasp of his huge hand. Between them they heaved the Gael up out of the gaping blackness, Cormac aiding them with a twist and a lift of his rangy form that swung his legs up over the brink.

"Thor's blood!" ejaculated Wulfhere, more shaken by the experience than was Cormac. "It was touch and go then. . . . By Thor, you still hold your sword!"

"When I drop it, life will no longer be in me," said Cormac. "I mean to carry it into hell with me. But let me look into this gulf that opened beneath me so suddenly."

"More traps may fall," said Wulfhere uneasily.

"I see the sides of the well," said Cormac, leaning and peering, "but my gaze is swiftly swallowed in darkness. . . . What a foul stench drifts up from below!"

"Come away," said Wulfhere hurriedly. "That stench was never born on earth. This well must lead into some Roman Hades—or mayhap the cavern where the serpent drips venom on Loki."

Cormac paid no heed. "I see the trap now," said he. "That slab was balanced on a sort of pivot, and here is the catch that supported it. How it was worked I can't say, but this catch was released and the slab fell, held on one side by the pivot...."

His voice trailed away. Then he said, suddenly: "Blood—blood on the edge of the pit!"

"The thing you slashed," grunted Wulfhere. "It has crawled into the gulf."

"Not unless dead things crawl," growled Cormac. "I killed it, I tell you It was carried here and thrown in. Listen!"

The warriors bent close; from somewhere far down—an incredible distance, it seemed—there came a sound: a nasty, squashy, wallowing sound, mingled with noises indescribable and unrecognizable.

With one accord the warriors drew away from the well and, exchanging silent glances, gripped their weapons.

"This stone won't burn," growled Wulfhere, voicing a common thought. "There's no loot here and nothing human. Let's be gone."

"Wait!" The keen-eared Gael threw up his head like a hunting hound. He frowned, and drew nearer to one of the arched openings.

"A human groan," he whispered. "Did you not hear it?"

Wulfhere bent his head, cupping palm to ear. "Aye—down that corridor."

"Follow me," snapped the Gael. "Stay close together. Wulfhere, grip my belt; Hrothgar, hold Wulfhere's, and Hakon, Hrothgar's. There may be more pits. The rest of you dress your shields, and each man keep close touch with the next."

So in a compact mass they squeezed through the narrow portal and found the corridor much wider than they had thought for. There it was darker, but further down the corridor they saw what appeared to be a patch of light.

They hastened to it and halted. Here indeed it was

lighter, so that the unspeakable carven obscenities thronging the wall were cast into plain sight. This light came in from above, where the ceiling had been pierced with several openings—and, chained to the wall among the foul carvings, hung a naked form. It was a man who sagged on the chains that held him half erect. At first Cormac thought him dead—and, staring at the grisly mutilations that had been wrought upon him, decided it was better so. Then the head lifted slightly, and a low moan sighed through the pulped lips.

"By Thor," swore Wulfhere in amazement, "he lives!"

"Water, in God's name," whispered the man on the wall.

Cormac, taking a well-filled flask from Hakon Snorri's son, held it to the creature's lips. The man drank in great, gasping gulps, then lifted his head with a mighty effort. The Gael looked into deep eyes that were strangely calm.

"God's benison on you, my lords," came the voice, faint and rattling, yet somehow suggesting that it had once been strong and resonant. "Has the long torment ended and am I in Paradise at last?"

Wulfhere and Cormac glanced at each other curiously. Paradise! Strange indeed, thought Cormac, would such red-handed reivers as we look in the temple of the humble ones!

"Nay, it is not Paradise," muttered the man deliriously, "for I am still galled by these heavy chains."

Wulfhere bent and examined the chains that held him. Then with a grunt he raised his axe and, shortening his hold upon the haft, smote a short, powerful blow. The links parted beneath the keen edge and the man slumped forward into Cormac's arms, free of the wall but with the heavy bands still upon wrists and ankles; these, Cormac saw, sank deeply into the flesh which the rough and rusty metal envenomed.

"I think you have not long to live, good sir," said Cormac. "Tell us how you are named and where your village is, so it may be we might tell your people of your passing."

"My name is Fabricus, my lord," said the victim, speaking with difficulty. "My town is any which still holds the Saxon at bay."

"You are a Christian, by your words," said Cormac, and Wulfhere gazed curiously.

"I am but a humble priest of God, noble sir," whispered the other. "But you must not linger. Leave me here and go quickly lest evil befall you."

"By the blood of Odin," snorted Wulfhere, "I quit not this place until I learn who it is that treats living beings so foully!"

"Evil blacker than the dark side of the moon," muttered Fabricus. "Before it, the differences of man fade so that you seem to me like a brother of the blood and of the milk, Saxon."

"I am no Saxon, friend," rumbled the Dane.

"No matter—all men in the rightful form of man are brothers. Such is the word of the Lord—which I had not fully comprehended until I came to this place of abominations!"

"Thor!" muttered Wulfhere. "Is this no Druidic temple?"

"Nay," answered the dying man, "not a temple where men, even in heathenness, deify the cleaner forms of Nature. Ah, God—they hem me close! Avaunt, foul demons of the Outer Dark—creeping, creeping—crawling shapes of red chaos and howling madness—slithering, lurking blasphemies that hid like reptiles in the ships of Rome—ghastly beings spawned in the ooze of the Orient, transplanted to cleaner lands, rooting themselves deep in good British soil—oaks older than the Druids, that feed on monstrous things beneath the bloating moon—"

The mutter of delirium faltered and faded, and

Cormac shook the priest lightly. The dying man roused as a man waking slowly from deep sleep.

"Go, I beg of you," he whispered. "They have done their worst to me. But you—they will lap you round with evil spells—they will break your body as they have shattered mine—they will seek to break your souls as they had broken mine but for my everlasting faith in our good Lord God. He will come, the monster, the high priest of infamy, with his legions of the damned—listen!" The dying head lifted. "Even now he comes! Now may God protect us all!"

Cormac snarled like a wolf and the great Viking wheeled about, rumbling defiance like a lion at bay. Aye, something was coming down one of the smaller corridors which opened into that wider one. There was a myriad rattling of hoofs on the tiling—"Close the ranks!" snarled Wulfhere. "Make the shield-wall, wolves, and die with your axes red!"

The Vikings quickly formed into a half-moon of steel, surrounding the dying priest and facing outward, just as a hideous horde burst from the dark opening into the comparative light. In a flood of black madness and red horror their assailants swept upon them. Most of them were goat-like creatures, that ran upright and had human hands and faces frightfully partaking of both goat and human. But among their ranks were shapes even more fearful. And behind them all, luminous with an evil light in the darkness of the winding corridor from which the horde emerged, Cormac saw an unholy countenance, human, yet more and less than human. Then on that solid iron wall the noisome horde broke.

The creatures were unarmed, but they were horned, fanged and taloned. They fought as beasts fight, but with less of the beast's cunning and skill. And the Vikings, eyes blazing and beards a-bristle with the battle-lust, swung their axes in mighty strokes of death. Girding horn, slashing talon and gnashing fang found flesh and drew blood in streams, but protected by their helmets, mail and over-lapping shields, the Danes suffered comparatively little while their whistling axes and stabbing spears took ghastly toll among their unprotected assailants.

"Thor and the blood of Thor," cursed Wulfhere, cleaving a goat-thing clear through the body with a single stroke of his red axe, "mayhap ye find it a harder thing to slay armed men than to torture a naked priest, spawn of Helheim!"

Before that rain of hacking steel the hell-horde broke, but behind them the half-seen man among the shadows drove them back to the onslaught with strange chanting words, unintelligible to the humans who strove against his vassals. So his creatures turned again to the fray with desperate fury, until the dead things lay piled high about the feet of their slayers, and the few survivors broke and fled down the corridor. The Vikings would have scattered in pursuit but Wulfhere's bellow halted them. But as the horde broke, Cormac bounded across the sprawling corpses and raced down the winding corridor in pursuit of one who fled before him. His quarry turned up another corridor and finally raced out into the domed main chamber, and there he turned at bay—a tall man with inhuman eyes and a strange, dark face, naked but for fantastic ornaments.

With his strange short, curved sword he sought to parry the Gael's headlong attack—but Cormac in his red fury drove his foe before him like a straw before the wind. Whatever else this high priest might be, he was mortal, for he winced and cursed in a weird tongue as Cormac's long lean blade broke through his guard again and again and brought blood from head, chest and arm. Back Cormac drove him, inexorably, until he wavered on the very brink of the open pit— and there, as the Gael's point girded into his breast, he reeled and fell backward with a wild cry. . . .

THE TEMPLE OF ABOMINATION

(Outline)

"Easy all," grunted Wulfhere Hausakliufr, "I see the glimmer of a stone building through the trees—Thor's blood, Cormac, are you leading us into a trap?"

The tall Gael shook his head, a frown darkening his sinister, scarred face.

"I never heard of a castle in these parts—the British tribes here abouts don't build in stone—it may be an old Roman ruin—"

Wulfhere hesitated, glancing back at the compact lines of red-bearded, horn-helmed warriors. "Maybe we'd best send out a scout—"

Cormac Mac Art laughed jeeringly. "You barbarians still start at the name of Rome, and Alaric led his Goths through the Forum fifty years ago. Fear not, there are no legions in Britain—I think that is a Druidic temple. We have nothing to fear from them; we are moving against their hereditary enemies."

"And Cerdic's brood will howl like wolves when we strike them from the west instead of the south or east," grinned the huge Dane. "It was a crafty idea of yours, Cormac, to hide our dragon-ship on the west coast of Britain and march straight through British country to fall on the Saxons. But it's mad, too."

"There's method in my madness," responded the

Gael. "I know that there are few warriors hereabouts; most of the chiefs are gathering about Arthur Pendragon for a great concerted drive. Pendragon! He's no more Uther Pendragon's son than you are. Uther was a black-bearded mad-man—more Roman than Briton and more Gaul than Roman. Arthur's as fair as Thorfinn there, but there's no hint of red in his hair and beard. And he's pure Celt—a waif from one of the wild western tribes that never bowed to Rome. It was Lancelot who put it into his head to make himself king."

"Is he smooth and polished like the Romans were?"

"Arthur? Ha! One of your Danes would look like a gentlewoman beside him. He's a shock-headed savage with a love for battle." Cormac grinned ferociously and touched his scars, "By the blood of the gods, he has a hungry sword! It's little gain we reivers from Erin have gotten on his coasts!"

"Would I could cross steel with him," grunted Wulfhere, thumbing the edge of his great axe. "What of Lancelot?"

"A renegade Gallo-Roman who has made an art of throat-cutting. He varies reading Petronius with plotting and intriguing. Gawaine is a pure blooded Briton like Arthur, but he has Romanesque leanings. It's absurd to see him aping Lancelot—but he fights like a blood-hungry devil. Without these two Arthur would have been no more than a petty chieftain. He can neither read nor write."

"What has that to do with it?" rumbled the Dane. "Neither can I—there's the temple."

They had entered the tall grove in whose shadows crouched the small squat building, that seemed to leer out at them from behind a screening row of columns.

"I thought these Britons were mostly of a new sect called Christians," growled Wulfhere.

"The Romano-British mongrels are," assented Cormac. "The pure Celts hold to the old gods, as we of

Erin. By the blood of the gods, we Gaels will never turn Christian while one Druid lives."

"What do these Christians?" asked Wulfhere curiously.

"They eat babies. What else, I do not know."

"But the Druids burn men in cages of green wood."

"A lie spread by Caesar and believed by fools," rasped Cormac impatiently. "Wait here—I'm of the same belief as these Britons, if I am of a different race. These druids will bless our expedition against the Saxons. I have little faith in their mummery, but it might help—"

The Gael strode between the columns and vanished. Wulfhere leaned on his axe; it seemed to him that from within came a faint rattle—like the hoofs of a goat on a marble floor.

"This is an evil place," muttered Thorfinn. "I thought I saw a strange face peering about the top of a column a moment agone."

"It was a funguous vine grown and twisted about," contradicted Hrothgar. "See how the fungus plants spring up all about the temple, how they twist and writhe like souls in torment—how human-like their appearance—"

"You are both mad," broke in Hakon Snorri's son. "It was a goat you saw—I saw the horns that grew upon its head—"

"Thor's blood!" snarled Wulfhere. "Be silent! Listen—"

Within the temple had sounded the echo of a sharp incredulous cry; the rasp of a sword from its scabbard, a strange slithering sound. Wulfhere glanced uncertainly about, then gripped his axe and started for the portals. From between the columns came Cormac Mac Art. The cold was gone from his face and his eyes stared like a man who has looked into dark, nameless gulfs. Wulfhere's eyes fixed themselves on his sword and widened in slow horror. That blade was stained to the hilt with a green, leprous slime.

The Gael gestured toward the interior of the temple.

"Take your wolves in, Wulfhere," he said, "and let them loose—"

The Skull-splitter nodded stolidly and nodded to his warriors. With a clank of mail and a shimmer of axes the Danes strode into the temple. Cormac stepped out away from the columns and drew in a deep breath of pure air. He glanced at the writhing, snaky vines that clustered close and a strong shudder shook him. From within came an incessant clangor of steel, muffled blows—blows that sank deep in strange flesh. There was a frantic drumming as of many goats racing back and forth across the tiles. Once there sounded a strange cry that was partly like the death howl of a human, partly like the dying bleat of a goat, partly like the rending creak of a vine torn away.

Cormac wiped his forehead where the sweat beaded. "Not a Druidic temple—" No—not a temple where men deified the cleaner forms of Nature—creeping, crawling shapes of red chaos and howling insanity—slithering essences of blasphemy lurking like loathsome reptilian things in the ships of Rome—ghastly growths that spawned in the ooze of the Orient transplanted to cleaner lands—rooting themselves deep in good British soil—grisly pre-Druidic oaks that fed unnameable monstrosities beneath a gibbous moon. And the legends were true—slime of a decadent Greece writhing among ancient abominations—the goatlike satyrs, mandrake—and a culminating horror—a ghastly cult older than Atlantis—vines and human beings and goatish monstrosities that interwove and twined together—that set aside natural laws and mingled plant, beast and human in nameless creation.

Anthropoid, leprous shadows loping down colossal black basaltic corridors of pulsing, inhuman night. Mowing slavering abominations of an Elder World squatting on a lone bare hill in a grisly ring, howling brain-shattering incantations to a hag-moon. Titanic shapes of blasphemy and gibbering madness growing out of the night and silence of a midnight oak forest.

Age-forgotten gods that ground writhing howling naked humans between their brutish jaws.

Wulfhere came from the temple with his Vikings behind him. To Cormac's questioning glance he shrugged his gigantic shoulders.

Cormac sheathed his sword with a clang; again he breathed deeply.

"On to Wessex," he growled. "We'll clean our steel in good Saxon blood."

POUL ANDERSON

Poul Anderson is one of the most honored authors of our time. He has won seven Hugo Awards, three Nebula Awards, and the Gandalf Award for Achievement in Fantasy, among others. His most popular series include the Polesotechnic League/Terran Empire tales and the Time Patrol series. Here are fine books by Poul Anderson available through Baen Books: